DATE DUE

soldier sister, fly home

soldier sister, fly home

nancy bo flood
illustrations by shonto begay

Charlesbridge

Poem on pages 106–107 by Emily Dickinson, originally published in *Poems*, ed. Mabel Loomis Todd and Thomas Wentworth Higginson (Boston, MA: Roberts Brothers, 1890).

Text copyright © 2016 by Nancy Bo Flood
Illustrations copyright © 2016 by Shonto Begay
All rights reserved, including the right of reproduction in whole or in part in any form.
Charlesbridge and colophon are registered trademarks of Charlesbridge Publishing, Inc.

Published by Charlesbridge
85 Main Street
Watertown, MA 02472
(617) 926-0329
www.charlesbridge.com

Library of Congress Cataloging-in-Publication Data
Flood, Nancy Bo, author.
Soldier sister, fly home/Nancy Bo Flood.
pages cm
Summary: Half-Navajo, half-white sisters Tess and Gaby are separated when Gaby drops out of college to join the army. Now as Gaby is deployed to Iraq, she asks Tess to care for Blue, the spirited horse that Tess dislikes. Tess struggles with her identity and with missing her sister, and she decides to spend the summer with her grandmother at sheep camp where tragedy strikes.
ISBN 978-1-58089-702-0 (reinforced for library use)
ISBN 978-1-60734-821-4 (ebook)
ISBN 978-1-60734-822-1 (ebook pdf)
1. Sisters—Juvenile fiction. 2. Navajo Indians—Juvenile fiction. 3. Families—Arizona—Juvenile fiction. 4. Horses—Juvenile fiction. 5. Arizona—Juvenile fiction.
[1. Sisters—Fiction. 2. Navajo Indians—Fiction. 3. Indians of North America—Arizona—Fiction. 4. Family life—Arizona—Fiction. 5. Horses—Fiction. 6. Arizona—Fiction.]
I. Title.
PZ7.F668So 2016
813.6—dc23 [Fic] 2015018819

Printed in the United States of America
(hc) 10 9 8 7 6 5 4 3 2 1

Display type set in Leaf and Leaf Filled
Text type set in Aboriginal Serif and Aboriginal Sans by Chris Harvey
Color separations by 5000K Inc. in Pembroke, Massachusetts, USA
Printed by Berryville Graphics in Berryville, Virginia, USA
Production supervision by Brian G. Walker
Designed by Martha MacLeod Sikkema

To the memory of Lori Piestewa,
and to all the women in the military
who put themselves in harm's way

Feathers fly,
Carrying a heartbeat.

Fly home.
Blue Horse, Łį́į́' Dootł'izhii.

prologue

raven's lament

The last time I shot a rifle, I was ten. Dad picked me up after school, and we headed to the rifle range just outside Flagstaff.

We drove along Route 89, the four-lane highway that runs down the long slope of the San Francisco Peaks like a frozen gray river, straight into the hot, dry belly of the desert. The Navajo Nation. My home.

I liked being at the range with my dad. I liked the kick of the rifle, the way the explosion vibrated through me and shook the sky. The burning smells were raw and real. I had a steady hand. A sharp eye. I liked it all.

Gaby, my older sister by six years, never came with us to the rifle range. Gaby hated guns. My sister looked Navajo, like a woman warrior with gorgeous long hair. I looked white. Some kids at school didn't believe we were sisters and said I was lying about being half Navajo. But we were both tall, with champion-fast running legs.

No one else was at the rifle range that day, just Dad and me and one big old raven. It always showed up. *Craawk!* It sat hunched over on top of a light pole, head cocked, and watched. Reminded me of Gaby—watching, thinking, and then speaking her mind.

A shiny new pickup drove in, stirred up a whirl of dust, and stopped next to us. The front door opened, and a big white guy hauled himself out of his truck, lifted out his rifle, stood and stared, made me nervous.

Craawk! The raven didn't like him either.

I took careful aim at the farthest target, pulled the trigger, and shot a bull's-eye.

"That ain't real shooting, but maybe not so bad for a girl."

The man held up his rifle. He glanced at the target but then stared at that big old bird. The raven stared back.

I should have shouted, waved my arms. I didn't do anything. I didn't even move.

One shot. *Bang!*

A cloud of red dust puffed up beneath the pole. Black iridescent feathers lay in a heap. The raven's eyes, still open, staring, surprised.

I didn't even move.

The man walked over and kicked it. "Dumb bird. Not even good for eating."

I swore right then that I'd never shoot a rifle again.

That was three years ago. Now my sister is the one carrying a rifle.

chapter one
fallen warrior

Before dawn, Grandpa stepped into the kitchen. I had gotten up in the dark to take an early-morning run. Grandpa looked at me with eyebrows raised, then lit the kerosene lantern rather than switching on a light. I slipped on my running shoes, stopped, and waited.

Grandpa reached for his rifle from above the doorway, handling it as carefully as if it were one of Grandma's newborn lambs. He sat down and reached for a flannel cloth and a can of oil. With a slow, steady rhythm, he rubbed oil into the dark wood. It was beautiful to watch.

Light from the lantern flickered across Grandpa's face. He reached into his shirt pocket, took out an arrowhead, and placed it on the rifle. He repeated several phrases in Navajo, sat silent for a moment, and then returned the arrowhead to his pocket.

Grandpa revered his rifle nearly as deeply as Grandma did the sunrise.

Slowly he stood up, straightened out his stiff joints. I stepped out of the way as he replaced the rifle above the door.

"Going running?"

I nodded. "I won't be late."

He looked at the round white clock over the sink. "Watch the time, Teshina. This memorial is important."

"If I'm not back when it's time to leave," I said as my hand tightened around the door handle, "go ahead without me."

"This memorial is for Lori, for her family." He cleared his throat. "We all need to be there."

My glance met his. Neither of us said another word.

I stepped out and eased the door shut, careful to not make a sound so it wouldn't wake Mom. She'd worked the late shift at the hospital in Tuba City and had returned home only a few hours ago. I looked up at my bedroom window. I had always shared that room with my sister. But not anymore. Not since everything had changed.

Already the sky was brightening from dark to gray. Soon streaks of red would appear and a haze of gold would pour over the sagebrush and drifts of sand. Then the sun would lift over the mesa's edge and start warming up the day. So many times my mother's mother—my *shimá sání*—had reminded me that each sunrise was sacred, a gift, a time to greet the Holy Ones, a time to receive their blessings.

As always, Grandma had gotten up long before dawn in order to be outside facing east, ready to greet the sunrise. Afterward she began hauling hay and water to her herd of goats and sheep. I walked toward the corral, my steps cushioned by the soft sand. The air was still cool and full of good smells—sweet green hay, smoke from the cook fire, and the sour odor of livestock. Grandma turned, her face brightening as I waved. She continued with her work, tossing handfuls of grain to her animals, calling each by name, scolding the troublemakers. Apricot was easy to spot because of her rust-colored wool, but also because she was always nudging close to steal an extra mouthful of grain. Grandma laughed, pushing Apricot away from the feed bucket. Old Jack, with his long scraggly beard, shoved his head in as soon as Apricot's head was out. Grandma pulled Jack away and tossed oats to both of them. Then she gave an extra handful to Betty. I smiled. Grandma had nicknamed that goat Betty-Boobsy because Betty made more milk than any other three goats combined.

I waved again and kept on walking, past the horse shed and the horse corral. Blue was circling round and round, kicking up dust and whinnying his complaints. I shook my head. I hated that horse. He was mean to everyone except Gaby, and he was hotheaded and stubborn. It was his fault that my sister's ankle had gotten smashed. That translated into no more running track, no more trophies and blue ribbons. My sister lost all chances for a college sports scholarship. Then what did she do? She dropped out of college and enlisted in the army—how stupid was that?

My stomach did a flip-flop. We didn't need any more fallen warriors around here.

A curve of sun broke over the mesa's edge, and I was still staring at Blue. *Get moving, Tess. Stop thinking about stuff you can't change. Run!* I breathed in, said a little prayer to the spirits just in case they really were listening, and took off. My body started to feel alive, and my mind quieted. I looked to the horizon and ran full out. Someday I'd run all the way to Elephant Feet. Gaby had promised to race with me. Nonstop. But now my sister isn't running—she's marching. My throat started getting tight. *Stop thinking, Tess. Just run.* A steady rhythm settled in, my legs reaching, arms pumping. Breathe. Run. Nothing else.

The horizon shimmered as if the Holy Ones were pouring out their blessings. Running worked its magic. My heart pounded, and I was flying. Running free. Running and wishing I'd never have to turn around. *I don't want to go to the memorial. Not this one, not today.*

I stopped. Breathing came in fast gulps. I yelled to the sky, "Gaby, why aren't you here? Lori was your friend!" Overhead a raven swooped low, cawing as if scolding me. I stopped. Breathing . . .

I kicked at the sand, turned, ran slowly back home.

Mom, Gramps, and Grandma, dressed in their best Navajo attire, sat around the kitchen table, sipping coffee, waiting. As soon as I opened the door, Mom glanced at the clock. No one said a word.

I rushed through a cold shower, threw on some fresh clothes—my good jeans and the Western shirt Mom had washed and ironed the day before. I hurried outside. Mom had loaded the truck bed with gifts for Lori's family. Grandpa sat in the front on the passenger side, his fingers tapping the sill of the rolled-down window. Grandma sat in the middle. Dad was missing—still in Phoenix, working overtime. He had transferred to Phoenix when Gaby started college. Not that he wanted to, but it meant a higher position in the computer department and more pay. When Gaby found out, she threatened to drop out of college and get a job. Both Mom and Dad had snapped back, "Don't you dare."

Well, she *had* dared and dropped out. But not for a job.

I climbed into the back of the truck, sat down, and off we went.

The truck bumped along the rutted driveway. Red dust swirled behind us. We turned onto the main road, and my insides got jumpier.

I sat upright, my back pressed against the cab window, and watched the long highway unwind. It felt strange sitting in the truck bed all alone. Usually Gaby and I sat huddled next to each other, singing silly songs and telling goofy jokes, like when we were younger. Riding in the truck bed was our special time. Even after Gaby left for college, every Friday after school I'd ride along with Mom to Flagstaff. We'd do some shopping, pick up Gaby, then head back home. I'd talk nonstop for a while, filling her in on all the latest Rez gossip. For the entire drive it was just the two of us with the wind whipping by.

Once when I was little, Gaby had leaned in close and said, "I've got a secret—promise not to tell?" Of course I had promised.

"I have a boyfriend and he kissed me, a big long kiss."

She had grinned. "Tess . . . I liked it." She had a ridiculous look on her face. "We're going to do it again."

As soon as we had gotten home, I hopped out of the truck and told Mom. I didn't want my sister kissing some slobbery boy. Gaby hadn't spoken to me for a week. Finally I had written her a long poem about my sorry, sad heart. Even then I had to agree to do her share of dishes for an entire month.

Tuba City came into view as we drove over the final set of hills. Not much to see. Up ahead was the one shopping center—a grocery store, a pizza place, Frank's Dry Goods store, and a Chinese takeout restaurant. Rows of government housing—identical, tan-colored houses with blue metal roofs—lined the streets. All along the barbed-wire fences, shreds of white grocery bags flapped like broken-winged birds. Our truck slowed, and we turned just before the post office, where the US flag flew at half-mast.

My stomach did another flip-flop. Half-mast. For Lori.

Traffic was backed up, a long line of pickups and SUVs. We inched along to the school and finally parked in one of the last remaining spaces.

Mom climbed out and hurried around to help Gramps and Grandma out of the truck. I didn't move. Mom frowned at me. "Teshina, it's time."

I swung myself over the side of the truck. Grandma patted my hand. Then she looked at Mom. They often said a lot to each other without saying a word. Gaby and Mom were like that too.

Car doors slammed shut. No one spoke. No one shouted hello. An uneasy quiet hovered over the parking lot. I followed my family into the gym.

I felt the drums before I could see them.

Their vibrations echoed through my bones.

Boom-BOOM! Boom-BOOM!

I felt scared, like when I was little. I wanted to reach up and hold on to my big sister's hand.

chapter two
purple blanket

Our family paraded single file along one side of the gym and up into the bleachers—everyone except for Grandpa. He was dressed in his full Navajo veteran regalia: his good jeans and official yellow-orange shirt, and he'd put on his string tie and his United States Marine Corps hat with gold initials—USMC—across the front. Grandpa strode straight to the front of the gym, where other veterans had gathered. As an honored warrior, one of the oldest veterans, and a World War II Code Talker, Grandpa would lead the procession.

The drums beat steadily—three large wide drums clustered together. Six or seven men sat circled around each drum. The gym buzzed with the murmuring of voices. Someone coughed. A baby cried. Suddenly the drumming grew louder, more demanding. The tempo accelerated, and the sound crescendoed to a final *boom-boom* beat. Silence. I glanced at my mother. Tears slid down her cheeks. Softly, very slowly, the drums began again. The people in the lowest row of seats stood. Then row after row, like ripples across a pond, we all rose to a stand. The men took off their hats. The procession began.

People stepped quietly, single file, forming a long line that soon circled around the gym. Everyone was dressed to show their respect, to give honor. The men wore stiff new jeans, Western shirts, braided bolo ties, polished boots, and broad-brimmed hats. Older women wore their traditional velvet-layered skirts, satin blouses, circles of silver and turquoise on heavy squash-blossom necklaces, and wide silver belts. White moccasins wrapped up past ankles and softened steps.

Each familiar face caused me to catch my breath. Miss Begay, my kindergarten teacher, had been Lori's teacher too. Mr. Yazzie, the high school basketball coach, stared straight ahead, his ashen face showing no emotion. Behind him walked Mr. Whitethorn, our art teacher, a champion rodeo rider, and Mrs. Goldtooth, the track coach, who had once told Mom that I showed great potential. After starting school in Flagstaff as a boarding student, I seldom thought about these people. Flagstaff was only an hour's drive away, but it was a whole different world—another planet, where I was always an outsider, an Indian, and, even worse, a mixed-blood. At school, I thought about survival, not about the Rez. My teammates called, "Hey, Navajo!" or "Move it, Pokeyhontas!" They never saw me. They never saw Navajo or white—they only saw an Indian.

I kept to myself. I sat alone in the cafeteria, always reading a book. I was invisible.

Here is home. These are my people. But I had left, and each time I returned, I felt more mixed up. Today was even harder than I thought it would be. Part of me wanted to be here, and part of me wanted to escape, even back to Flagstaff.

Row after row of people continued to file down the bleachers to join the circling procession. It was our turn. Mom took hold of Grandma's arm and helped her stand up. Shimá Sání looked small and wrinkled. She stood to full height, head high, shoulders back. It didn't matter that she barely came up to my chin. She was saying, *Yes, we can survive this. We have survived so much else.* Grandma had lost her oldest son and two of her brothers—fallen soldiers in previous wars.

The drums kept beating. *Boom-BOOM.*

My mother stepped forward, her hands clenched around the Pendleton blanket we would give to Lori's family. Lori and my sister had been friends here in Tuba. My sister was a few years younger and wanted to be a champion Little League player like Lori.

Lori's dad was an honored soldier, decorated with medals for bravery shown in battle in Vietnam. Gaby had said she wasn't surprised when Lori enlisted. Lori was the first of my sister's friends to join, the first to finish boot camp, the first deployed to Iraq. "Nothing fancy, nothing dangerous," Lori had emailed. "I'll help with supplies, help the soldiers who do the fighting. They're the real warriors. Before you know it I'll be back."

Then the news: Lori's convoy had taken a wrong turn and come under fire.

Missing in action: Lori Piestewa.

Then more news. Lori wasn't missing.

My sister's friend.

Specialist Lori Piestewa, 507th Maintenance Company, US Army.

First Native American woman to fall in combat on foreign soil.

Now, today, this memorial. Everyone, both Navajo and Hopi, had traveled from all the surrounding Rez towns—Shonto, Red Lake, Tonalea, Moenkopi, Tuba City. Lori was half Hopi, half Mexican American. Everyone knew Lori and her family.

Boom-BOOM. I wanted to run, race far away from death. I wanted to feel the tall canyon walls surround me, solid, not leaving, not changing.

Boom-BOOM. The beating of the drums would not let me go.

The stream of people circled the gym. The elders—the oldest veterans—led the procession. My grandpa, a proud warrior, marched with his shoulders back and head high. Then came the younger veterans from other wars. A young Hopi soldier watched from the side in a wheelchair, one leg missing.

I looked away, stared at the gym floor, newly polished. Only a few seasons ago, my sister stood there, center circle, crouching, waiting for the whistle to blow—ready to take the tossed basketball. Today she was far away, marching, rifle over her shoulder. Today Lori's mother stood in that circle, wrapped in a dark-purple blanket. Purple, the color of honor. *Fallen Warrior.* On each side of her stood two little children, Lori's children. Did they hope Lori would come home and surprise them?

They must hope that. Mothers don't die.

I joined the line of people flowing past, ashamed that I felt glad it wasn't my sister who was gone. That it wasn't my mother wrapped in a purple blanket.

My sister is alive.

But my sister had enlisted. All she had said was, "We are warriors, Tess. We help our country when help is needed. And we help our families." She had given me a hug. "Don't worry, I'm not getting deployed—it's boot camp and some maintenance company. Perfectly safe. I'll be back before you even miss me." She had laughed. "Except when you're washing dinner dishes!"

I closed my eyes and pictured the rifle above the door, my grandfather's solemn face. I saw that raven, limp in the red dirt.

I didn't even move.

My sister left, and I didn't stop her, couldn't stop her.

Perfectly safe. That's what you promised, Gaby: perfectly safe.

chapter three
cowboys and indians

The next morning Mom drove me back to Flagstaff, back to school. No one asked where I'd been. No one mentioned Lori's name. Flagstaff was a different planet than the Rez. It hadn't been my idea to transfer from Tuba City and finish junior high in Flagstaff. But Mom and Dad had said I'd get a better education and have more opportunities, especially in sports. I was breaking school records in both track and cross-country. Maybe I could get that scholarship my sister had lost. I had agreed to give a city school a try because Gaby was in Flagstaff too, a college student at NAU, Northern Arizona University. It would be *our* year, a year with no parents. We had big plans. Well, maybe not so big—eat pizza for breakfast, rent movies, stuff ourselves with popcorn. She'd come to my cross-country meets, cheer me across the finish line, and every time I came in first, double chocolate malts would be on her.

But she enlisted.

Now I was an Indian at a white school and alone in Flagstaff. My sister was hundreds of miles away, marching with a rifle at a fort in Texas. Not exactly how we'd planned our big year together.

Winter sports had ended. Spring meant track season at school, lambing and sheep-shearing season at home. Then a surprise email. Gaby had leave. She was coming home! In May or June at the latest. One whole week, maybe two—my sister was coming home!

The time crawled by like I was waiting for Christmas. The day finally arrived. Dad picked Gaby up at the Phoenix airport and drove directly home. I kept pacing, inside the house and out, staring at the wide empty stretches of sage and sand. A big old raven swooshed over my head. It seemed as if it was looking right at me. I glared back. *Are you bringing good news? My sister's coming home. For two whole weeks. Nothing's changing that.*

Just after sunset, I finally saw car headlights turn off the main road and bump from sagebrush to sagebrush down our drive. My sister was home!

I ran out of the house and stopped. I remembered that Gramps and Grandma should be the first to greet Gaby. That would be the proper Navajo way. I took one quick look to make sure it was Dad's truck and that it was still coming up the drive, and hurried back into the house.

We all stood in the kitchen—Gramps and Grandma, Mom, me. The door swung open. No one moved. No one said a word. Gaby stepped into the room and stood there, stiff and straight. She looked different, decked out in splotchy army fatigues. And there was something else. Her hair. It was sheared short. Hair that she had vowed she would never cut, dark hair that had hung past her waist, gone. Her face had changed too, sharper somehow. And serious. There was no silly grin or teasing sparkle in her eyes. Gaby looked from one face to the next. She greeted Gramps and Grandma, and she stepped toward Mom.

"Gabriella!" Tears glistened in Mom's eyes. Gaby dropped her duffel, rushed over to Mom, and hugged and hugged, both of them crying. It scared me. Mom never cried like that. Tears at Lori's memorial, but not many. Mom was always so Navajo about not showing much emotion. Finally Gaby let go of Mom and looked at me.

"Tess, you . . . you've grown. Not just taller. You're not a kid anymore."

"Your hair . . . I didn't know about your hair." What a stupid thing to blurt out.

"Oh, I forgot." Gaby ran her fingers through her hair and sort of smiled. "Seems like ages ago." An awkward silence. "Sorry. I don't know what to say. It's a big shift leaving base and being back here. Bigger than I thought."

Something broke loose inside me. I rushed across the kitchen and wrapped my arms around my sister. I needed to hold her, to make sure she really was right here. My sister was different, even smelled different. I let go and stepped back. We were both crying—happy, sad, maybe even scared. So many feelings, all jumbled.

I wiped my eyes with my sleeves and stuffed my hands in my pockets. Gaby glanced at the clock. A few minutes ago my head had been full of questions. *Boot camp, what was it like? Tougher than anything she'd ever done? Were any of the other recruits Navajo? Did she get teased about being half Indian, half white? Did she miss the Rez? Did she miss us?* So many questions, but I didn't ask even one.

Blue whinnied from the corral. Gaby grinned like her old self and looked out the window. "Guess someone else needs a hello." She glanced at Dad. "Is it OK if Tess and I go down to the corral?"

"Sure. We can talk later." Something was troubling Dad. I could tell by the way his jaw was working from side to side.

"The serious stuff can wait. Come on, Tess."

"What serious stuff?" No one answered. Something didn't feel right.

"Come on, let's have a little sister time." Gaby was already out the door, calling to Blue, and he was already whinnying back. This part of my sister hadn't changed—she loved her horse.

Gaby flipped the switch that lit the yard. Blue nickered as she rubbed his nose and gave him a handful of feed. "Here, Tess, make friends with Blue. Offer him some sweet oats, his favorite."

"No, thanks. Blue and I aren't exactly on the best terms. Blue hates me."

"No, he doesn't. He smells that you're afraid, and that scares him. Here, try this."

Gaby gave me a handful of grain, and we both held out

our hands, side by side. Blue sniffed Gaby's arm from her elbow down to her fingertips, snorting and sniffing until Gaby was laughing. He did the same to my arm.

"See, now he knows we're friends, that I trust you."

Blue ate both handfuls of grain and bobbed his head as if saying thanks.

Gaby laughed again. "Want to ride double?"

"It's dark."

"I love riding in the dark. It's like flying. Don't worry. Blue knows his way. Two sisters under the stars, riding across the desert. Come on, Tess, do it for me."

Gaby didn't wait for an answer. She slipped on Blue's halter and swung herself onto his back. "Stay right here. I'll give Blue a warm-up run, and once he settles, I'll be back for you."

She clicked her tongue and gave Blue a gentle swat with the rope. Blue half-reared, trotted a few yards, and switched to a steady lope. Gaby let out a holler, kept Blue at a steady pace, circled the corral, and disappeared into the dark. A couple of minutes later they reappeared. Gaby was smiling her old silly grin.

"Hey, little sister, Blue's ready." Gaby reached down, and I grasped her hand, quick-counted to three, and leaped as she pulled me up. I wrapped my arms tight around her waist. Suddenly Blue took off. My stomach lurched, and the world became a dark swirl of stars above and hoofs thundering beneath me. I started getting dizzy and then remembered—breathe! Gaby started singing some crazy Navajo song, sometimes giving a whoop or holler, and talking to Blue. I gripped tighter, breathed deeper, and closed my eyes. Now I could feel the smooth rhythm of Blue's steady galloping, galloping. I squeezed my sister and let myself fly.

Two sisters under the stars, riding across the desert.

Out of nowhere a coyote barked. It sounded close, as if it were right next to us. Another one howled from the other side, and then another. They sounded like they were all around us. Blue bolted.

Gaby yelled, "Hold on, hold on!" Blue ran full out. The coyotes' yipping and howling fell behind.

Gaby started talking low and steady, "Easy, boy, easy. Let's slow this race down." Blue swerved around a tumble of boulders that I could barely see. Gaby kept talking to Blue. I felt her leaning back, tightening the reins, and slowly, slowly Blue's pace slackened. Finally Gaby kept him at a gentle trot.

"Where are we?" I couldn't see lights anywhere.

"I have no idea. Blue does." Gaby patted Blue's withers, stroked his neck. "Home, Blue, take us home."

Gaby loosened the reins, let Blue have his head. He veered to the left and trotted along some unseen trail. A few minutes later we topped a small hill, and I could see the welcome glow of the yard light.

Gaby turned around and called over her shoulder, "Nice ride!"

And then we were at the corral.

My arms were still shaking from holding on so tight, and when I slid off Blue, my legs felt like rubber.

"Hey, want to go again?" Gaby turned around. She looked plain happy. "You did great. Remember, if something ever goes wrong, give Blue his head. Trust him. He'll take care of you."

"Trust that horse? Never. Not unless you're holding the reins."

Gaby didn't say anything, just raised her eyebrows.

She led Blue back into the corral. She held his head in her hands, put her forehead to his. Talked to him in Navajo. Funny, I swear he understood. It seemed like they always understood each other. Then Gaby became all business and gave him a quick rubdown and another handful of grain.

She closed the gate and stood and looked at Blue for a moment. "Maybe someday you and Blue will be friends." She started walking toward the house. "Come on, sis. It's time for me to talk with the folks. I promised Dad we'd have some time alone."

"Talk? About what?"

"I'll explain later."

"I guess that means I'm not invited."

"I guess you guessed right. Sorry about that."

Gaby's mood had shifted. She was focused on whatever the big talk with the folks was about. Her face was unreadable.

I trudged up to my room—our room—sat cross-legged on my bed, and pulled out a few comics. I stared at the covers. In the kitchen below, Mom, Dad, and Gaby were talking, so softly that I couldn't make out any words. Mom's voice was sharp, asking Gaby about something. There was a lot of silence. No one was moving around fixing dinner or getting coffee. My sister was home. For two weeks. No one was laughing. Something wasn't right.

chapter four
change of orders

I stared at my sister's empty bed. We had always shared this room. Until she left for college. Every night she wore her silly Mickey Mouse pajamas, bought with the money she'd earned watering corn and squash in Grandma's field. Twice a day she had carried two big buckets and given each plant one dipper full. At the end of that summer, our family had made a special trip to Disneyland, celebrating Gaby's "Best Runner on the Rez" trophy. Gaby had had just enough money to buy those pajamas after she got me a stuffed Pluto puppy. Pluto's head never stayed upright, flopping over onto his tummy, but I didn't care.

Our beds had matching tie quilts Grandma had sewn from Blue Bird flour sacks when Gaby started junior high and I began first grade. I chose the quilt with a bluebird singing in every square. Gaby chose the one with the words "Enriched," "Bleached," and "Cortez Milling Co., Inc."

Gaby had kept it a secret from our folks that she could barely read. Night after night she had traced the letters across the quilt, saying their sounds. Then she'd slowly read an Archie comic. I had taught myself to read, but that was my secret. One night I opened a brand-new comic and started reading it to her. Gaby burst into tears. She had been getting ready to start junior high, and I could already read better than she could. So we had made a deal. Every night we would read a different comic together. That was the summer my sister learned to read.

My hair never grew as long as Gaby's. I loved her hair—black, thick, and smooth. Just like Mom's. My hair was boring brown like Dad's and never grew longer than halfway down my back. After our evening showers, Gaby would sit on the edge of her bed. I would sit behind her and brush her hair until all the snarls were combed out. Gaby had said she'd never cut her hair. Never.

Finally I heard my sister's footsteps coming up the stairs.

"Ready for a talk, Tess?"

"Sure." My sister looked tired, and something else too. Determined?

"There's plenty of stuff I want to explain." Gaby pulled the door shut. "I'm sorry."

"Sorry?"

"I've got some hard news, and I want you to hear it from me."

My heart began racing. "News about what?" All kinds of thoughts started jumping around in my head.

"Be patient with me tonight, OK, sis? Words keep getting stuck in my throat."

I stared at the bluebird singing away in the middle of a quilt square.

"Mom told me about Lori's memorial. I know it wasn't easy for you. Thanks for being there."

I yanked loose a piece of yarn from the quilt and twisted it around my finger. Twist, untwist.

Gaby hesitated, then started again. "Remember how every November on Veterans Day Grandpa rides horseback across the mesa with all the other veterans? How proud he is dressed in his Marine Corps regalia?"

I frowned. "If you have bad news, then just say it. Why are you talking about this other stuff?"

"Dad told me Grandpa led the procession at the memorial."

In my mind, I saw those two little children standing next to Lori's mom. The purple blanket. I felt the beating of the drums inside me.

"Remember how Grandpa would take out his war medals? Let us watch when he polished them? He was a hero. A Code Talker."

"Stop talking in circles, Gaby. Whatever it is, just say it!"

My sister didn't answer. She just sat on her bed, slowly tracing every letter in "flour."

"You're still mad that I enlisted." She looked at me. "I want to explain—"

"Going to college. Becoming a doctor. Those were your dreams. Healing people, not killing them."

"Thanks a lot."

I bit my lip. "Sorry. I didn't mean—"

"Losing that scholarship was hard, Tess. Really hard." Gaby looked at me, her eyes angry. "Not being able to run and win. Mom and Dad having to pay my tuition and everything because of that stupid accident. I hated it."

"It was Blue's fault. Why didn't you get rid of him?"

"It was never Blue's fault. I pushed him too hard. I didn't trust him, and he knew it."

That nightmare moment came back as if it were just happening. Rodeo finals, barrel racing. Blue had refused the turn. Gaby had flown right over him. The crack of bone. My sister's leg twisted at a terrible angle, her face in the dirt. I had run into the arena, but someone pulled me back. Ambulance lights flashed, and a stretcher had carried my sister away. One broken leg, a smashed ankle, and all her dreams of being a track star, her scholarship, gone.

"You didn't have to drop off the team."

"I couldn't win, Tess. Couldn't even place."

"But quit college?"

"Plans sometimes take a detour, Tess."

"Detour! Joining the army is not exactly a detour."

"Would you please shut up and listen—"

"You can't make Lori come back."

"Listen to me. Just *listen*! This has nothing to do with Lori!"

"Then what does it have to do with?"

"It has to do with another change." Gaby stopped, stared down at the quilt. "My unit is being sent to Iraq, Tess. Deployed."

Our eyes met. I felt cold, empty.

"Deployed? When?"

"Soon."

The room began to shrink smaller and smaller. "You can't. It's not fair."

"Dad's known since he picked me up at the airport. I just told Mom. She's pretty shook up. They went over to the hogan to talk with Grandma and Gramps." Gaby swallowed. "I waited until now . . . so I could tell you myself."

"You promised. You said—"

"Tess, stop! Listen to me, please."

The drumming grew louder, filled my head. I stared at my sister. "Deployed? No. Not like Lori."

"I promise, Tess, not like Lori. They took a wrong turn. Lori tried to protect her fellow soldiers." Gaby stopped, shaking her head. "Lori was a true warrior, Tess."

I looked at my sister. "Is that what you want? To be some war hero? Dead or alive?"

"No, that's not what I want."

"Then what do you want?"

"What do I want?" she snapped back. "I don't know. To pay my own way—medical school, college tuition. It's all jumbled up." Gaby shook her head. "I'm trying to figure it out, Tess, how to be me. Navajo? White? What's me?"

"You? What about our family? And being here? Isn't

that being you? All those promises you made? What about that?"

"What are you talking about?"

"You said we'd have time together—"

"I'm sorry, Tess."

"Sorry? What good's saying sorry? You enlisted, and I said that was stupid, and you said the army would send you somewhere safe."

"I didn't know, Tess."

"You didn't know? That's all you can say? You don't know shit!"

"Tess!"

Neither of us spoke. Everything seemed blurry, out of focus. Neither of us moved. Finally Gaby stood up, walked over, put her arms around me.

"I am sorry, Tess. Nothing is the way I planned it. Getting my leg hurt. Losing all possibility of a scholarship. I was trying to make the best decision, not just for me, but for our family. My orders got changed. Sometimes we have to do what we swore we'd never do."

I stared at my sister. She looked so tired, so sad. I tried to smile.

"I guess that's why Mom always says 'Never say never.'"

Gaby gave me a squeeze.

I squeezed her back, and held her in a long, scared hug. I closed my eyes and listened to the drumming of my sister's heart.

Then Gaby took a deep breath, stepped back, and stared at the floor. "Tess?" She didn't say anything more. Instead she glanced at the window—the one that looked out at the corrals.

"What, Gaby?"

"Never mind."

Finally my sister looked at me. "There's something important I need to do. I'll be back soon."

I stood by the window and watched as she walked toward the barn. I knew where she was going. She needed to tell Blue.

Someone knocked on the bedroom door.

"Come in. I'm still awake."

Mom came in and sat down on the edge of my sister's bed. "Gaby's deployment. She told you?"

I nodded.

Mom swallowed. "We're going to have a ceremony. A protection ceremony. For soldiers heading to war."

War. Going to war.

"She has to leave sooner than we thought, Tess."

"What?" I looked at Mom. "What are you talking about?"

"Gaby didn't tell you? She has to leave . . ." Mom looked away.

"When?"

"In just a few days."

"But she has two weeks of leave. That's what she said."

"I'm sorry, Tess. When her orders changed, her leave was canceled. She was lucky to get these few days."

"Lucky?" I didn't even try to keep the sarcasm out of my voice.

Mom didn't look at me, but she continued talking. "I'll need your help, Tess. Everyone in the family will be here."

I stared at Mom. “But she promised. Two weeks! This isn’t fair.”

I wanted to grab my sister, hold onto her, shake some sense into her.

Mom stood up and looked at me. “I’m sorry, Tess. We’re all upset.”

I didn’t move. I didn’t answer.

“Want to talk some more?”

“Not tonight.”

“Then get some rest. Tomorrow will be a busy day.” Mom put her hand on my shoulder, and gave it a squeeze. “It’s a lot to take in, I know.”

chapter five

hózhǫ́, walk in beauty

The sky was just beginning to lighten, just enough to wash away the stars. Sunrise was still an hour away, and before I was needed to help with preparations, I claimed this first hour as my own.

I looked over at Gaby's bed. She hadn't come back from the barn. She was probably sleeping there. That's where she liked to go when she was upset, surrounded by the smells and sounds of horses, sheep, and goats. Curled up in a cozy nest of saddle blankets on top of a big pile of hay.

Two days. I have two days to be with my sister.

Before the ceremony. Before she leaves.

I opened the top drawer of my dresser and pushed back a pile of papers, poems that had been stuck in my head until I had written them down. Beneath the poems was an envelope full of sticky notes, mostly funny messages from Gaby, and a torn-out piece of newspaper. A photo. Why had I saved it? *Please, no more fallen warriors.*

Lori Piestewa, smiling in uniform.

The caption read, "First Native American Woman to Fall in Combat."

I picked up another piece of paper, a letter from Gaby. The first one she sent after arriving at boot camp. Maybe it was a poem. Or a prayer. It said only this:

Shideezhí, *little sister,*
Walk with me, in harmony, in beauty.
Little sister, let me fly.
Hózhǫ́,
Walk in Beauty.

"Walk in beauty? *Me* walk in beauty? *Hózhǫ́,* walk in beauty yourself!" That frightened me. Saying these words out loud. What if the spirits were listening? Gaby believed in them. Especially the *Yé'ii.* Mom said that autumn was when the *Yé'ii* might appear before leaving for their winter's rest in the mountains. Gaby would often ask me to come with her to town in hopes we'd see them.

The *Yé'ii* scared me. When I was little, Gaby and I were standing outside the Tuba City Trading Post when two tall men wearing turquoise masks had begun dancing around us, shaking red rattles right in our faces.

Gaby had wrapped her arms around me. "Don't be

scared, Tess. When the men put on their masks, they become the *Yé'ii,* the Holy Ones. Watch."

I had held tight to my sister's hand. The *Yé'ii* laughed, making sounds I didn't understand, and offered us candy. Gaby nodded and said to me, "It's OK, take it." I hid my hands behind my back. Gaby took the candy for both of us.

"The *Yé'ii* protect us, Tess. See, they even give us candy. Chocolate, my favorite. One night after it snows, we'll gather around a big bonfire, and the *Yé'ii* will dance the Night Chant. Then they'll leave for the mountains by Flagstaff and rest there for the winter."

Gaby had let me eat all the chocolate.

Yé'ii, *will you protect my sister now?* I wanted some sign, a message, something that said, *She'll be fine.* Did I expect a raven to land on the windowsill, maybe an eagle feather to drop out of the sky?

I shoved the papers back into the drawer, slipped on my running clothes, and hurried out the door. Outside I could breathe, and the world felt normal. I needed to stop thinking. I needed to run.

Grandma was already at the sheep corral. Lambing season was in full swing, and every few hours, day and night, she checked the new lambs and the pregnant ewes. Once the lambs were strong and shearing was done, Shimá would take her herd down into the canyon for the summer, where there'd be plenty of water and grass. Gaby always went with Grandma because she loved being in the canyon. I had gone too, a few times, but only for a couple of days each time. The canyon was so big, and it sort of freaked me out. Except one place that I loved: a narrow side canyon with a waterfall—Gaby's waterfall. Gaby said there was magic in that canyon, that it was a place the spirits liked to visit. I believed her. Who would go with Shimá Sání this year? Had my sister thought about that?

Grandma waved for me to come over. She was bottle-feeding an orphaned newborn lamb.

Shimá looked at my running shoes, nodded. "Good. We each find our way. Your sister is finding hers. Yes. Run."

I jogged past the pasture where Dad kept his two prize beef cattle, Tuition One and Tuition Two. Dad had been socking away "cow money" since Gaby started high school. If I kept my grades up, trained hard, and ran fast, maybe I could get the scholarship Gaby had lost. Then when Gaby returned, she wouldn't have to worry about tuition money. She'd have veteran's benefits, and I'd have a scholarship. My sister wouldn't have to reenlist. Dad wouldn't need to work so far away in Phoenix or keep raising cattle to pay for tuition.

I stopped, faced east, stared at the horizon, and whispered the words Grandma said every morning. *Hózhǫ́*, walk in beauty, in harmony. Me? I was walking in mud. That made me smile, even laugh a little. Shimá would be pleased. She has always said that laughter is healing.

I stretched, pressed my hands against the sand. It felt good to touch the earth.

OK, Tess, get out of your head. Run!

The sharp red line of the mesa cut straight across the horizon as if a kid had drawn it with a ruler and colored it in with a crayon. The flat red mesa extended for miles until it was interrupted by huge sandstone monuments that stuck straight up like giant stone sculptures.

As I ran, the whole world became desert, only this desert. Every run, every morning, was different. Skinks and other lizards zipped out of the way. Ravens whooshed overhead, the sound of their wings close. I'd glance up, call out, and sometimes they'd answer. Once I ran past a gathering of ravens, dozens of them hunkered on the limbs of a big gnarly pinion tree like old men arguing politics. In early summer, hummingbirds buzzed past or soared straight up, fifty feet or more, to dazzle their girlfriends with straight-down dives. Tiny cactus wrens startled me when they'd burst from a bush like fireworks. A jackrabbit might freeze for a moment, with its tall radar ears perked straight up until—zoom, a streak of furry gray, and presto! Gone!

Now as I ran, dawn changed to day. The sun poked above the horizon. Light spilled across the mesa. I stopped.

"OK, Holy Ones," I whispered, then I closed my eyes and listened to the slight breath of wind. "If you are out there, please protect my sister. Can you do that?"

chapter six

promises

I ran hard all the way back, and didn't stop until I was in front of the barn. Blue took one look at me, snorted, and trotted to the far corner of his corral.

Blue. I remembered the first time my sister saw Blue. Dad had driven up pulling a horse trailer. He had stepped out of the pickup with a big wide grin on his face. Gaby and I had watched as a gray-blue stallion had backed nervously out of the trailer, looked around, and then whinnied, his long neck vibrating as he trumpeted. He was beautiful! He had the sturdy build of a quarter horse and the graceful lines of an Arabian. Dad had seen Blue at auction and couldn't resist. He'd been looking for a stallion for Mom's mares. Mom kept a few mares at our place for riding, but most of her herd roamed free in the canyon. Dad said the canyon mares needed some new blood for breeding. Mom had agreed, and Dad was always happy to look over livestock at local auction.

Gaby had taken one look at Blue and broken out with a smile nearly as wide as Dad's. She marched right over to Blue. Putting one hand on his trembling side, she spoke to him in Navajo. She looked at Dad. "Can I have him?"

"I don't know. He's a handful," Dad said, taking off his hat, scratching his head. "He's got some mustang in him. Might make him a bit wild and unpredictable." Dad looked at Blue and then at Gaby. "He'll take a lot of training."

"I can do it!"

Gaby stroked Blue's neck. He quieted. She rubbed between his ears, talking softly to him all the time. They'd had some kind of special bond ever since.

I walked over to the horse barn and opened the door. No Gaby, but I could see where she had made her hay nest with a bunch of saddle blankets. I picked up Blue's reins, a bar of saddle soap, and a cleaning rag, and a can of mink oil. I grabbed one of Blue's bridles and sat down. The horse barn—more of a shed than a barn—was a good place to be in the summer, dark and cool, full of horse and hay smells. Smells that went with my sister. Many hot summer afternoons we had spent in here with a stash of comics, trying to keep out of Mom's sight. Mom was always ready with a list of chores that needed doing.

I liked helping my sister with her horse stuff. I didn't care what—brushing, grooming, even holding on to a hoof while she dug out gravel with the hoof pick. After getting the tack ready, Gaby would brush Blue, then lunge him in a big wide circle in the corral, cantering him in one direction and then the opposite, making sure he picked up the right lead. I'd stay in the barn and thumb through a stack of old comics, starting with my least favorite, Wonder Woman, saving Archie, with my favorite character, Veronica, for last. The barn was a good place for thinking. It was where I wrote my best poems. I always kept my journal and a handful of pencils and a sharpener under a particular hay bale. I'd write stuff I didn't want anyone to see, even Gaby. I tried writing mirror image and backward like da Vinci, but the problem was, I couldn't read any of it.

Eventually Gaby would whistle for help setting up the barrels. Then she'd work Blue, running him full out, guiding him with the press of her legs, shifting her weight, teaching him to turn tighter. Maybe knock another tenth of a second off their racing time. Finally she'd reward him with a handful of sweet oats and take him out on the mesa and let him stay in a smooth easy lope. When they returned, they'd gallop straight toward me—Gaby with a big grin on her face and her long hair flying wild.

But with me, Blue could be plain mean. He might bite or kick, and once he had rolled in a muddy creek when Gaby and I were riding double. Oh, Gaby had gotten mad!

Once after an especially bad day, I had asked her, "Why do you put up with that horse?"

"I'm not a quitter. If I work him right—slow, steady,

and firm—he could be a champion. Anyway, Blue's bad behavior is my fault. If I'm scared, it makes him jumpy. That's when I have to pay attention to what he's saying, slow down, and be firm." Gaby grinned. "Remember that time he bit me? I grabbed the feed bucket and bonked him on the head hard enough to let him know I meant business. He never tried that again."

"With you."

"You have to show Blue who's boss."

"Blue knows who's boss, and it isn't me."

"Mean what you say, Tess. He'll listen." Gaby laughed. "Just like we do when Mom gives orders."

Orders. That thought pulled me right back from daydreaming. *Now the one giving orders is the army.*

I poured a bit of mink oil on the scrub rag, placed the bridle across my knees, and scrubbed. Blue's saddle would be spotless. Gaby would like that.

Blue nickered from the corral. Gaby must be around.

The door creaked open. "Tess, you're here! I was looking all over for you," Gaby said. "You're harder to find than a lost sheep!" We both laughed. Gaby smiled just like her old self. My sister was home.

"Did you talk to Mom this morning?" she asked.

"Not yet. Did you?"

"We had coffee. With Dad."

"How are they doing?"

"Better. A lot better." Gaby studied my face. "And you?"

"I had a good run."

"Hey, nice job on the saddle." She paused. "I really am sorry, Tess. Sorry we won't have time for more night rides, for being together. I was hoping you and Blue would begin to sort of like each other."

I didn't answer. I stared at the cloth in my hand.

"Tess, I'll be gone a long time. A year, maybe more."

"A year!"

"Blue's going to be lonesome. He'll need attention, someone to ride him. Mom and Gramps said they'd help with the feeding. But Blue will go crazy if he's cooped up in that corral all the time."

"Then sell him."

"I'd never sell him. Never! He's a special horse, Tess. You know that." Gaby waited until I looked up. "Will you take care of him?"

I stared at my sister. *She knows how I feel about Blue.*

Gaby's tone softened. "Teshina, will you do this for me? Ride Blue. Until I'm back."

"Why did they change your leave? Just like that? It's not fair."

"It's an emergency deployment. I was lucky to get these few days."

"Right. Real lucky." I hated the mean sound in my voice, hated it. But words kept jumping out. "Why did you sign up in the first place? Trying to be a war hero? Trying to be Navajo?"

"I *am* Navajo, Tess. Same as you!"

"Wrong! We're mixed-bloods, half-breeds. Misfits. Kids at school remind me every day."

"I've told you, Tess—ignore them. They'll stop."

"It doesn't work that way for me. You're the gorgeous Navajo princess. I'm the kid who looks like a mixed-up mutt."

"Stop it, Tess. Maybe when you start seeing yourself for who you are, who you want to be, and—"

"Is that why you're heading off to war?"

"Haven't you heard anything I've tried to say? When I get back I'll be a veteran, Tess, with benefits. I'll finish college and pay for *everything* myself, everything. I've been figuring it all out ever since Lori . . ."

"Since Lori what? Enlisted? Got killed? Finish saying what you mean."

"Stop right there, little sister. You know better than to talk about death. Talk can make things happen."

I put my head in my hands. Why was I being so stupid? I shook my head and muttered to my sister, "You know I'm scared of that horse."

"I do know that. But I don't know who else to ask, Tess. There's no one else I trust." Gaby put her hands on my shoulders. "But I shouldn't have asked. It wasn't right of me."

I never could understand it, but my sister loved her stupid horse.

"Just one thing more." Gaby tried to smile, but mostly sadness showed. "Run for me. It's the running I miss. I loved crossing that finish line first. But even more I miss running with you—flying over the red rock, slogging up sand dunes. I miss it—running wild with my sister."

"I miss it too."

"I don't want to leave feeling like you—"

"I'll take care of Blue."

Gaby opened her mouth to say something, but stopped.

"You heard right. But you stay safe, big sister. That's

your part of the bargain." I sort of smiled. "And I'll take good care of your damn horse."

"This is a different finish line, Tess. I'll cross it. And I'll come home."

chapter seven
protection ceremony

Gaby and I hardly saw each other the rest of that day. Mom kept us both busy with an endless litany of stuff that had to be done exactly right for the ceremony. More relatives and friends kept arriving and bustling around our place like bees buzzing around a hive. People I didn't even know drove up, unloaded gifts of food, asked what else was needed. *Time!* I wanted to shout. *Time with my sister!* Instead I smiled and mumbled something sort of polite.

All these people around, asking the same questions: *When does she leave? Where are they sending her? Do you feel proud?* I needed to get away from the endless chatter. I needed space. Instead I was handed job after job to do. Then it was dark, no time to even eat supper. No time to think. I was so tired, I fell into bed, closed my eyes, and was gone.

The next morning I slept past dawn. Missed greeting the sun. I hoped the Holy Ones wouldn't hold it against me. The protection ceremony would begin at dusk. I'd been to a lot of ceremonies and sings but never a protection ceremony for soldiers. My sister a soldier? She hated guns.

Shimá was busy cooking. Several big pots of stew bubbled on the kerosene stoves set on makeshift tables in the kitchen. Dad stayed outside, splitting logs for the all-night fire. That's what I wanted to be doing. Hold on tight to an ax handle, swing it up, and *whack!*—split that sucker. An entire night's supply of wood had to be split and stacked exactly according to the medicine man's instructions. *Hastiin* Dághaatsoh would arrive sometime late in the afternoon to check that everything had been prepared correctly. I've always liked *Hastiin* Dághaatsoh, and I especially liked that his name meant "Mr. Big Mustache."

I felt like I was walking around in someone else's skin. Or someone else was inside mine. I usually liked being part of all the relatives bringing food, cooking, talking, sharing gossip. Usually my job was raking the sand around the hogan until it was smooth and spotless. After the sun dipped below the horizon, the medicine man would enter the hogan, followed by Gaby, our grandparents and parents, and then the other relatives.

It's hard to stay awake all night during a ceremony, to sit up straight, to not doze off. But being there was beautiful—

a long night of listening to chanting, being part of a sacred mystery. I usually felt wrapped in a safe cocoon, breathing in the smells of earth, wood, and fire. Aunts and uncles, some I didn't even know, would sit cross-legged with their backs to the hogan's earthen wall, no one speaking. We'd all face the center, where the medicine man sat, the place of honor. Sometimes a sudden pop from the cedar fire would startle me. Dad was usually at ceremonies too. Even as a white person, a *Bilagáana*, Dad was welcome. Someone would whisper about Dad's Vietnam combat medals, and someone else would mention Dad's generosity. Everyone brought gifts of groceries to a ceremony. Dad brought the most. Elders always commented, and then Mom would sit up extra straight.

Once everyone was settled, the medicine man would hold up a cedar bough with the needles burning and wave an eagle feather, wafting the smoke in each of the four sacred directions. He would begin the prayers. All night we would mostly listen, sometimes speaking out loud our worries and prayers. At dawn, as people left the hogan, everyone would receive a gift of food. A morning feast would be ready—huge pots of lamb stew, piles of fry bread, charcoal-grilled mutton, and all the food brought by relatives. Laughter and talking would spill out like the warmth of the morning sun spilling over the canyons.

But tonight's ceremony was different. Tonight's ceremony was for a soldier going into combat. For my sister.

I didn't want any part of it.

Gaby stayed busy visiting with relatives, so I returned to the house. It was a relief to be in the kitchen. No one expected me to talk. Mom saw me walk in and raised her eyebrows, her way of asking for help. I walked over to a huge mound of white dough. Mom nodded as if to say thanks. I began patting pieces of dough into balls for making fry bread. Grandpa strolled into the kitchen. He sniffed one bubbling pot and then another.

"Smells mighty fine in here. Maybe you want some professional sampling."

Mom looked up from the mound of peeled potatoes and smiled at her dad. "Sampling is not what's needed. What we need is mutton for grilling."

"That's exactly why I'm here, getting my knife." Grandpa reached to the highest shelf of the cupboard, took his long steel knife from its leather sheath, and tested the edge. No one ever touched that knife except Grandpa.

He looked at me. "Want to come along, Tess?"

Usually the thought of butchering sent me scooting far away, but today everything felt different. "Sure."

I followed him outside. Grandpa sat in a spot of shade under a tall old cottonwood. He began sharpening his knife.

"You doing all right today?" Gramps asked without interrupting the long careful strokes of the knife along the sharpening stone. "Kind of hard to take in all that's happening."

"Maybe."

Grandpa kept right on talking. "The night my brother left for war, I hid. I didn't come out until the next day. Even my dog couldn't find me."

"You didn't say good-bye?"

"I was mad."

"Didn't even go to his ceremony?"

"I wanted no part of his leaving."

I thought about what Gramps had just confessed. "Were you sorry you weren't there?"

"Sorry? Yes. Later on. But at the time, hiding was what I needed to do. Now that I think about it, a lot of years later . . ." Gramps sort of chuckled. "You could say I was scared. Up one side and down the other. Scared."

Grandpa pushed back his wide-brimmed hat. "I even thought that maybe I wasn't a real Indian. Maybe not a real brother." He put the knife in its sheath and then stood up. "We learn more from our mistakes than from what we do right. Nothing wrong with that."

Grandpa walked over to the sheep corral and pointed to the small ewe with the marked ear.

"That's the one your grandma chose. Bring her to me, Tess."

I climbed over the fence, dug my fingers into the sheep's thick wool until I had a good strong grip, and tugged her over to the gate.

Grandpa picked up the sheep and gently set her down in the truck bed. He tied her legs together with baling twine. "Good. Let's go."

I sat alongside the young ewe, cradled her head in one arm, and talked to her while rubbing the smooth spot between her eyes. The ewe stopped struggling.

Grandpa drove slowly over the bumps to an area a short way north of the hogan but far enough from all the buzzing activity. He spread out a small tarp under a cottonwood, slipped his knife under one edge, and set a small white pail next to the knife. He nodded to me and said, "Help me bring the sheep here."

I climbed out of the truck, and together we lifted the sheep and carried her to the tarp. She stayed calm, didn't fight us at all.

I sat down next to the ewe and placed her head on Grandpa's lap. This ewe was a pretty little thing, with a sweet triangular face and floppy ears that hung past her eyes. She didn't move. She lay there quietly.

"Is it hard?"

"To kill an animal, Tess? Is that what you mean?'

"Seems like it would be hard."

"All life is sacred, Tess. We give, we take. All part of the journey. It's OK not to like this part."

Grandpa stroked the ewe's neck. "Sometimes what needs doing is hard. Hurts."

He rubbed the top of her head, and his fingers moved down the length of her throat. He kept talking to the sheep, almost singing, as he massaged her neck, working the wool away from the place where a big vein ran just beneath the skin. The sheep didn't bleat, didn't struggle.

He spoke softly. "She must not feel fear. The knife stays out of sight so it does not frighten her. We thank this sheep for giving us her life. We ask her spirit to give strength to your sister."

I looked at the ewe's sweet face. *Give my sister strength, protect her. I want to believe you can do that. And I thank you. With all my heart, I thank you.*

Grandpa continued stroking the sheep's neck while extending her head. His touch kept her calm. Unafraid.

"Aaaah, yaaah, yah. Yes, we sing as life comes into this world," he said softly. "We sing when life travels out." Grandpa reached for the white pail and placed it under the ewe's neck. He slipped the knife out from

under the tarp and held it over the dark line of the blood vessel. Nearly motionless, he pressed the edge of the knife through the skin. Blood seeped along the thin cut. The ewe didn't even startle. A red stream flowed from the incision into the white pail. Grandpa kept talking until the ewe stopped breathing. Life gone.

"All life is sacred, Tess. Life given, life taken. Each in its own time."

Swiftly he removed the sheep's head, then cut through the skin down the belly, the legs, around the hooves. Fast. Almost bloodless. As if slipping off a woolly coat, he removed her skin in one whole piece and handed it to me. "Lay it on the ground, wool side down."

Grandpa cut the meat into chunks and placed the pieces on the skin. "First the meat rests. It will dry quickly in the sun, before we bring it to the kitchen."

Grandpa folded up the tarp and handed it to me. "This goes back in the truck." He picked up the pail. "I will finish the gutting, take care of the innards, and bury the sheep's blood so her strength will continue. That is my job."

When he was finished, Grandpa walked back to where the meat was spread across the skin. "You did well, Tess. All those questions inside you. No matter how far you run or where you hide, the questions follow." He paused. "But sometimes we need to run."

Piece by piece, Grandpa turned over each chunk of meat. "And we always need to eat. Which reminds me: I'm hungry enough to eat a sheep." Grandpa chuckled at his own poor joke. "And sometimes we need to laugh." Grandpa scratched his head and smiled. "Done. We're ready for your grandmother's inspection."

In the center of the kitchen, Grandma was calling out

orders as the tempo of cooking grew faster and faster. Mom was usually the one in charge, either as head nurse at the ER or head cook at home. But not for this ceremony. Shimá was the oldest woman in our family. She had the most authority, the most respect. Shimá was in charge.

"Those tougher pieces, they go in the stew pot. Add some fat. Keep stirring."

Shimá sorted through the rest of the meat. "Here, Tess, take these ribs. Beautiful." She handed me a roll of butcher paper. "Wrap them. They go in the refrigerator. After the ceremony we will give them to the medicine man."

Finished, I walked outside. Dad was stacking the last of the wood. Two of my younger cousins were raking the sand that skirted the hogan. Everything looked tidy. Cars were parked in a neat row along the corral. Where was my sister? What was she thinking? The sun was low on the horizon; the last of this day's light glowed golden over everything. I returned to the place of the butchering. Sat under the same tree. The odor of blood was still heavy in the air.

Life to death to life. A ceremony for warriors.

Gaby, you hate rifles.

During the ceremony Gaby will glance from face to face looking for me and be disappointed. But Grandpa will know.

All those questions. No matter how far you run or where you hide, the questions follow.

But sometimes we need to run.

I did need to run, to be alone. I stood up, glanced at the house and hogan, and turned the other way. I jogged along the path that zigzagged up the mesa wall behind our place, picked my way over the loose rock and boulders, and scrambled to the top.

I stopped, leaned over, and gulped air. Once my breathing returned to normal, I jogged along the cliff edge until I found a good lookout place. Gaby and I used to sneak up here, careful to stay out of sight because it was forbidden territory. Too many rattlers, too many crumbly edges to fall off. So of course it was our favorite place. One summer Gaby had brought a pack of cigarettes. We smoked, coughed, felt sick, and pretended to love it.

I looked over the ledge. A hundred feet below were my home and family, like a distant world. *Maybe I should go back down. No. Right now, this is where I need to be.*

Night settled in. The air cooled. Light drained from the sky. No moon would appear until much later. This high-desert world was quiet. Sometimes I could almost hear—or was it feel?—the low murmur of chanting below. I closed my eyes, and when I opened them a long time later, the whole sky was shimmering with stars. The Milky Way spilled across the darkness from horizon to horizon. The universe had never felt so immense. And I so small.

Red sparks from the fire inside the hogan swirled upward, sputtered, blinked out. I breathed in the sweet smell of cedar smoke and sat up.

Gabriella was in that hogan. My heart ached. I wanted to understand. Sometimes life was so strange.

My sister is a soldier. She will carry a rifle. A sheep was sacrificed for her to give her strength, to keep her safe.

I'll do anything to keep my sister safe, even slaughter a sheep.

Even take care of Blue.

chapter eight
sing to the *yé'ii*

I lay down, wrapped my jacket around me, and was surprised that the next time I stirred, I could hear the chatter and chirping of birds. The sky was beginning to brighten. Already dawn was beginning.

I stood up, brushed the sand off, and scrambled down off the mesa. I waited outside the hogan so Gaby would see me as soon as she stepped out. I wanted her to understand.

Aunts and uncles appeared. Finally my sister. She looked pale and tired. But she stood tall and looked straight ahead as she walked.

"Gabriella?"

"Tess, I missed you. Are you all right?"

I nodded, but before I could say anything, a clump of

younger cousins swarmed around her, talking all at once, asking questions. I watched as they escorted my sister to the house.

After I helped serve breakfast, there was nothing more I needed to do. I slipped up to my room. I opened the bottom drawer of my dresser and took out a teardrop pendant made of white shell and turquoise, framed in silver. I whispered a few words to the spirits or whoever might be listening and wrapped the pendant inside a sheet of parchment on which I'd written a sort of poem:

Red rock walls
hold turquoise sky.
Canyons change,
walls fall,
what stays?

I ask the Holy Ones:
hold you safe,
fly you home.

I slid the pendant and an Archie comic into the side pocket of Gaby's duffel. She had everything packed and ready to go.

My sister leaves today. She leaves today, and she will have this white shell and turquoise for protection.

I glanced at the clock and hurried outside.

"Hey, nice to see you, stranger. Where've you been?" Gaby called from the corral.

A thousand things I wanted to say. I walked over to my sister with my hands stuffed in my jeans pockets and didn't say any of them.

Gaby stood by the horse corral, talking to Blue, rubbing between his ears. For a minute she just stood there and stared at her horse, but then she turned and looked at me. "Got a minute? Right now. It's almost time for me to leave."

"I'm sorry."

"About what, Tess?"

"About your ceremony." I kicked at the ground. "About not being there."

We walked side by side to the barn. Gaby hung up Blue's halter, looked around at everything, her eyes holding on, then letting go.

"I'll be honest. It felt sad not to have you there. But it's OK. It really is. Gramps and I talked about it some. I think I understand." Gaby took a deep breath. "Hey, little sister, thanks again for taking care of Blue."

I shrugged. "Sorry I can't go with you down to Phoenix. There's only room for three in the pickup, and I know Mom wants to ride along with you and Dad."

"I was hoping that we could have that ride together. Like old times."

"I asked Dad, and he said no way. No riding in the back of the pickup on the big highway. I thought it was kind of funny."

"Funny? What do you mean?"

"He said it was way too dangerous."

"What's so funny about that?"

"You're going off to war. Isn't that sort of dangerous?"

I'd kept a really serious face, but then we both broke out laughing. So silly, but laughing together felt so good.

Gaby rumpled my hair like she did when I was little. "Listen, Tess, the next time I have leave, it'll be a longer one. We'll run at dawn. Me on Blue, you on foot. Like we talked about. All the way to Elephant Feet and back. If you can run that far."

"Hah. No problem. And what's my prize when I win?"

"Chocolate malts for both of us."

"Make that double chocolate."

"It's a deal." Gaby held up her palm, and we slapped hands. Then she said, "Ride him."

"Ride Blue? Never. I'll exercise him, lunge him till he begs for mercy. But I won't ride him."

"OK, OK, fair enough. But keep running, little sister."

"You come home."

"I will. All the way home."

Then it was time.

We all stood alongside the pickup—Mom and Dad, me, Grandma and Grandpa—and we watched as Gaby pushed open the kitchen door and lugged her duffel to the truck. She wouldn't let anyone help.

"Sit in the middle, next to your dad." Mom nodded to my sister. "I'll ride shotgun."

Dad looked at me. "Sorry you can't come too, Tess."

"It's OK. Anyway, it's best if I stay here," I said. "There are a dozen ewes that have yet to drop their lambs. Grandma could use some help, especially with all the extra hay and water that need hauling."

And then my sister left.

Gabriella texted me from the Phoenix airport:

Next time, sis, flying like the wind, two sisters. Promise.

I texted back a poem.

Ten little Indian
girls
grew up.
One became a doctor,
two work in Phoenix,
three went to college,
two got married,
one was a
warrior.
And the last
little Indian,
a soldier-girl Indian,
ran, ran, ran, all the way,
all the way
home.

All the rest of that day, I avoided going into the empty house. Finally it was dark. I was tired and needed to get some sleep.

An eagle feather lay on my pillow. Its quill was braided with thin leather ties, and next to it was a note: *When you are ready to fly.*

I reread the note and placed it with the feather next to my pillow. I didn't even change my clothes—just lay down, wrapped Shimá's quilt around me, and fell asleep.

The rattling of a gourd startles me. The rattling starts out soft, then grows louder.

A *Yé'ii* stands in the doorway.

His leathery face is painted turquoise. Black feathers fan out around his head like a halo—a dark, feathery halo.

He keeps shaking his bloodred rattle while dancing around me.

I am holding the eagle feather, and I walk toward the *Yé'ii.*

We face each other on the sidewalk in front of the Tuba City Trading Post, where I bought a chocolate bar—dark chocolate—for Gaby when she comes home. I hold the chocolate bar in my hand.

The *Yé'ii* shakes his red gourd, and his mask towers above me.

I hold out my hand. "Here, take it."

His eyes peer through narrow slits. His mouth is an open circle, but he doesn't speak.

"Take it," I say again. "Keep my sister safe."

The *Yé'ii* laughs. He shakes his bloodred gourd and takes the chocolate. Good. He takes the chocolate.

chapter nine

flunk!

I had two more weeks of classes in Flagstaff, and then the school year was done. Track season ended, the one good part of school. I was named "All-Around Best in Track," but getting that award didn't make me any friends like I was hoping it would. Some kids accused me of cheating and said that I'd gotten some weird Navajo magic from a medicine man. How can anyone cheat at track? And there's nothing weird or magic about medicine men.

In the hall by the lockers, girls clustered in tight bunches, already jabbering about the summer ahead, giggling, making plans, exchanging cell phone numbers. That left me out. The cell phone service on the Rez was intermittent and unreliable. Most of the time I had to stand on top of a sand dune near our house to get reception. Even then, I could text but not talk. Internet meant a trip to Tuba City to the tiny outreach library or the new espresso café. But it didn't matter, since no one asked for my number. And no one said anything about my soldier sister in the army, overseas, deployed. No one. I couldn't get out of that white school fast enough.

But home felt lonely without my sister around.

First day of summer vacation. Dad was back in Phoenix, Mom was working, Grandma and Gramps had gone to the Crossroads flea market to get a load of hay. I wandered down to the horse barn. It felt better than hanging around an empty house. Blue left me alone, and I left him alone, except to make sure he was OK. No scratches, no limping, and I checked that he had fresh water, clean hay, enough feed. He was antsy to get out of the corral. I knew I should exercise him, but I wasn't ready. But I had promised my sister. Maybe . . .

I stood next to the corral. Blue seemed to know that something was different. He trotted over to the fence, nickered, and looked at me.

"So if we go for a short walk—I lead, you follow—you promise to behave? No rearing, kicking, or running off. Tell you what: I'll give it a try, and if you behave, then I'll take you out for an evening stroll every day until sheep camp. Did Gaby tell you about sheep camp? Lots of mares down there in the canyon at sheep camp. Yep, you'll have fun. Next week you'll leave with the sheep."

I felt stupid talking to a horse, but hearing the sound of

a human voice, even my own, made the place feel less empty. I also felt guilty thinking about Shimá trying to manage the sheep, her horses, and Blue by herself, taking them all down to the canyon. But my sister was the one who should feel guilty, not me.

Blue bobbed his head, ears twitchy and flattened back. I stepped away from the fence.

"I know you're mad. You're tired of being cooped up in that corral." I tossed a flick of hay over the fence. "Sorry. I'm doing the best I can."

Blue snorted at the hay, nosed it, pushed it away, and snorted again. I liked this less and less.

I eyed the rope halter Gaby had left hanging on a fence post. If I could get it over his head, I could lead him out of the corral and walk him around for a while.

Show him who's boss. Don't let him know you're afraid. Good advice, Gaby, but you forgot to tell me how.

I had an idea. I got my sister's riding jacket and put it on. Maybe if I smelled like my sister it would help. I held the halter in one hand and reached over the railing with my other hand full of grain, careful to keep my palm flat. "Here, have some. My peace offering, sweet oats. Your favorite."

Blue trotted over. He sniffed the jacket from cuff to shoulder and snorted out a puff of dusty snot.

His ears went back again. I should have known. But I kept my hand flat, even though it was shaking, and stuck it under his nose. He sniffed the oats and scarfed up every kernel.

I breathed out, started to relax. Saw Blue's big teeth, but too late.

"What the hell?"

Blood dripped.

Blue snorted, spun around, and trumpeted his victory.

That sucker bit me. I can't believe he bit me.

Ride him? Never.

Maybe Gaby will flunk deployment camp. Some soldiers do.

Flunk, Gaby, flunk.

I took off Gaby's jacket, threw it in a corner.

Why did I ever say I'd take care of your dumb horse?

I quit.

A *craawk* scolded from overhead. I looked up.

No sign of a raven.

Black feathers lay in the dust.

chapter ten

a real indian

The days were huge and empty. Gaby was still gone. I got out a stack of old comics, flipped through a few, but tossed them back on the pile. After lunch Grandma asked me to go with her to Tuba City. She had some business to do, plus grocery shopping for sheep camp. I was happy to ride along. Usually Gaby drove Grandma into town. Today Grandma drove, even though she could barely see over the steering wheel or reach the floor pedals.

Two girls, one my age and one much younger, stood and watched as I helped Grandma step out of our old red truck.

In town when I spoke to my grandma, I addressed her

in formal Navajo, *shimá sání*, to show my respect. Today she was dressed in the traditional clothes she wore when she went to town on important business—blue velvet layered skirt, matching blouse, her turquoise necklace, and, of course, her modern white ankle socks and her favorite lime-green sneakers.

"Look, a real Indian!" the younger girl shouted, pointing at Grandma. "Look, Meggie, is she a real Indian?"

I hoped Grandma didn't hear her.

Shimá reached back into the truck to get her rug. She was bringing it to the trading post before she took her sheep down into the canyon for the summer. The rug was rolled up, wrapped in flannel, and tied with twine.

"I can carry that for you."

Grandma shook her head. I knew she would. She didn't even trust Mom to handle her prize rugs.

"She really is an Indian."

"*Shhh*, Becca, and don't point. It's rude."

I tried to ignore the little kid's remarks, but I recognized the older girl's voice. They stood side by side in front of the trading post, right where we were going. The older girl was from my school in Flagstaff. Megan. She was in my math class. She was smart, pretty, and popular. *Great, just my luck.*

I looked down. Maybe she wouldn't recognize me. I scooted to the other side of Shimá, took her arm, and pretended to help her across the parking lot.

"Can I take your picture? I've never seen a real Indian before." The younger girl held up her camera and pointed to it, I suppose in case we didn't understand English. I shook my head and guided Grandma faster toward the trading-post door.

"Tess?" the older girl asked.

My face flushed, and I smiled one of those polite I-wish-I-could-disappear smiles.

"Tess, I didn't know you lived . . . here."

"Oh, hello, Megan. Sorry, I didn't recognize you."

"Are you visiting, ah, relatives?" Tess looked at my grandmother.

"No." I looked at her confused face. "You were right the first time. I live here."

"We're shopping for jewelry," the younger girl blurted out. "Indian jewelry." She kept right on talking. "Look at that necklace, Megan." The younger girl pointed at Shimá Sání's squash-blossom necklace. "Is it real?" Then she giggled. "And those shoes!"

Megan tugged at the girl's sleeve. "Becca, hush."

Why was I embarrassed? I hated feeling this way—ashamed. Who wanted to be like these stupid white girls?

Me. That's who.

It was the same at school: part of me wanted to be one of those girls, and part of me wanted to stay invisible. Maybe my folks were right; maybe I was getting a better education. But what they didn't understand was that I was also getting a different kind of education.

"Hello, I'm Rebecca." The younger girl pushed in front of Megan and held up her camera. "One picture? OK?"

"Oh, sorry, this is my little cousin. Her family is visiting from Boston." Megan turned and frowned. "Rebecca, please stop being so rude. Tess is a friend."

"She's your friend? A real Indian?" Rebecca's eyes grew wide. "Do you live in a tepee?"

"Do you live in a log cabin?" I asked. "Come on, Shimá Sání, Mr. Snow is waiting." I reached for the door.

Grandma didn't move. She motioned for Rebecca to come closer. Rebecca's eyes grew even wider, and she looked at Megan.

Megan nodded. "Go ahead."

Grandma held up her turquoise pendant. "Yes, it's real. Sterling silver, very old, made by my grandfather and given to my grandmother. For many years it was hidden in a secret place like buried treasure with all our silver and turquoise. That was during the Long Walk. Probably you don't know about all that. In the trading post are interesting books about Navajo." Shimá Sání slowly smiled. "Yes, we are real Indians. More correctly, I am Navajo, Diné."

Rebecca stared, didn't say a word.

"You want a photo?" Grandma asked.

Rebecca glanced again at Megan. Megan raised her eyebrows. "It's OK."

"Give your camera to Teshina, my granddaughter. Rebecca, come over here." Grandma motioned for Rebecca to stand next to her.

"Teshina, take our picture. One real Navajo grandma and one real white girl." Shimá's eyes were twinkling. Rebecca handed me her camera and stood near Shimá. I snapped a few pictures and handed the camera back.

"Enjoy your visit here, Miss Becca and Miss Megan. Sorry we don't have more time to talk. We have business to get done in the trading post."

I took Grandma's arm and moved toward the door.

Grandma ignored my tug. "Good that we met, Miss Becca. *Hózhǫ́*." She held out her hand to Rebecca, who smiled and returned the handshake. "Now we both walk in beauty, in harmony." Finally Shimá Sání turned and stepped out of the bright sunlight into the air-conditioned quiet of the trading post.

I felt as if I had barely escaped. Why? This was my home. The home of real Indians. Real Navajo. I looked at my grandmother. She was about as real as Indians came, but me? I wasn't so sure.

The manager, Mr. Snow, rushed over as soon as we walked in.

"Let me help you, let me help you. My, such beautiful ladies visiting today." He gave a little bow to Grandma and then to me.

Mr. Snow towered above us, smiling a huge smile with broad white teeth framed by a thick black mustache. As a little kid I thought someone got mixed up and gave him the wrong name. Mr. Snow always wore big black boots, black jeans, black Western shirt, and a wide-brimmed black hat. The only parts of him that were snowy white were the pearl buttons on his shirt and his teeth. He always had a smile, a genuine smile. He also always had a box of chocolates tucked under the front counter. With a polite bow, Mr. Snow presented a fancy-wrapped candy to Grandma and one to me.

Mr. Snow and Shimá exchanged the usual comments about the weather and everyone's health, and then both became quiet, their faces serious. The ritual of bartering began.

Grandma stepped over to the glass display case and unrolled her rug. She smoothed her hand across the entire top, and then stepped back. Mr. Snow studied the rug, looking at the overall effect of colors and pattern.

"Exquisite work." He clicked his tongue. "This rug is

truly one of your finest." Then he began a meticulous examination, counting the number of threads per inch, feeling for any irregularities. Grandma's weaving was well known and respected, sought after by collectors. One of her Wide Ruins rugs was displayed in the Heard Museum in Phoenix. Being a weaver of rugs: Did that make her a real Indian?

Shimá Sání was especially proud of this new rug, a large one, nearly six feet long and four feet wide. She had woven the Navajo Tree of Life, which was not actually a tree but a fully leafed corn plant. Its roots twisted through dark red earth, with slivers of turquoise between the roots. Deep green branches reached across the rug. A dozen different birds flew between the branches—bright yellow finches and red-winged blackbirds. Other birds sat perched on the leaves—bluebirds, small brown thrushes, and desert wrens.

Grandma and Mr. Snow spoke quietly in Navajo. The bargaining might take only a few minutes, or it could last more than an hour before both were satisfied. I listened hard, trying to understand their words, trying to push away that nagging question. Real Indian? What makes one a real Indian? I didn't go to my sister's ceremony, like a real Navajo. I didn't weave, never wanted to, and I didn't even speak much Navajo. Mr. Snow spoke fluent Navajo, and he was not a real Indian. He was *Bilagáana*, a real white.

Gramps had been a Code Talker, a real warrior, but he didn't go to his brother's ceremony. For a while he worried that he wasn't even a "real brother." Shimá could butcher a goat as quickly as Gramps. She could look at the sky and know when rain was coming. She could ride her horse across a mesa, find an injured sheep, and never get lost. Most Flagstaff kids didn't know a butte from a mesa or a sheep from a goat.

And me? What did I know?

Mr. Snow extended his hand. They had agreed on a price. Grandma shook it once, gently, the Navajo way, like a real Indian.

chapter eleven

espresso

As we left the trading post, Grandma stood for a moment, her hand shading her eyes from the bright sunlight. The girls were gone, nowhere in sight. "Teshina, remember that pointing is rude, especially if you are a real Indian." She laughed, but what was funny about that?

"Why didn't you tell that Rebecca girl about pointing, Shimá? Talk about being rude!"

I took Grandma's arm, but she laughed again and shook herself loose.

"No, Teshina. When someone looks down on you, listen and learn. Walk with them."

"I'd have given her a piece of my mind."

Grandma clicked her tongue like she did at a misbehaving sheep. "No, Tess, we choose. We can laugh or bite. Laughing is better for the belly." Grandma chuckled as she walked across the parking lot, right past our truck.

"Hey, where are you going? I thought we had to go straight home."

Grandma kept walking, right to a new little coffee shop, Internet Espresso. I hurried to catch up.

I hadn't been to this café since it had opened. Grandma walked right in as if she were a regular customer. "Coffee latte. Extra hot. Small."

"Latte?" I stared at my grandmother. "Grandma, you ordered a latte?"

She turned to me. "Want one?"

I shook my head. "I didn't know you liked lattes." I didn't know my grandmother knew what a latte was.

"Good coffee. Kind of pricey. Stronger than the cowboy coffee at sheep camp."

That was the first surprise.

Grandma paid for her drink and walked over to a computer.

"What are you doing?"

Grandma smiled.

I couldn't believe what she did next. Sitting in front of the computer, wearing her velvet skirt, satin blouse, turquoise jewelry, and green sneakers, my real Indian *shimá sání* logged onto the internet as if she'd been doing it all her life.

"Got mail," she announced.

If I had been holding a cup of coffee, I'd have dropped it.

"From Gabriella. For you too."

From: Gaby
Sent: June 14, 2003, 4:02 AM
To: Shimá Sání
Subject: Surprise!

Yá'át'ééh, Greetings, Hello Shimá Sání.
And Tess, surprise!

I bet you're staring with your mouth open. Nice joke, right?

Thanks, Shimá Sání. I can't wait for you to tell me about it.

Remember, just hit "reply," type your message, then hit "send."

But before you do, my message to Tess is below.

Hello, Little Sister,

See, I still have my terrific sense of Navajo humor.

Grandma could hardly wait to do this little shocker. She said she'd invite you to tag along when she brought her rug into town.

I know you are probably still upset about my signing up. It's OK.

I would have been plenty mad if my wise, wonderful older sister shipped off without much notice. ☺

Sometimes we have to leave home to find it.

That's something Grandma said once when I was helping

her find a few missing sheep. She said, "Most sheep stay with the herd. A few stray off, wondering what's over that next hill. Or maybe looking for home."

I told her, "Well, they sure are looking the wrong way."

She said back to me, "Maybe that's what we all do at first."

So where's home for someone like us, half white, half Navajo? I started thinking about what you said that night we had our big fight, about not feeling like a real anything. I remembered how it was when I was your age—junior high—when kids divided into separate herds. That's when the name-calling got worse. Now, just as you are facing all that, what does your big sister do but up and leave. I'm sorry, Tess.

Being Navajo. What's that all about? Weaving rugs? I was never into that part of being Navajo. But the sheep and goats—I even like the way they smell. Being on my horse, riding Blue, that's what I really love. Flying across the mesa. Is that Navajo? White? Or just me?

Someday I'll be a doctor for Navajo kids. Means a lot of tuition money. Being here, doing this, is one way I can help.

Thanks for listening. . . . Maybe what I'm saying is that your big sister is still wandering over that next hill.

How's Blue?

I love you, little sister.

Gaby

P.S. Thanks for taking care of Blue. Tell Gramps hello and tell Grandma I'm sorry she'll be heading down to sheep camp without me. That's a hard one. Tell Mom and Dad they raised me right, and I love them.

P.P.S. I keep the white shell and turquoise teardrop near me, always.

I rushed through whole sentences and then read every word again. I stared at the computer until Grandma cleared her throat.

"Oh, sorry. I guess it's your turn." I scooted out of the way.

Grandma hit "reply" and began to hunt and peck with two fingers.

My grandmother was sending email as naturally as herding sheep, weaving rugs, or flipping fry bread.

"OK, done." Grandma stood up to get her coffee refilled. "Your turn, Tess."

I logged into my own account and began typing.

From: Tess
Sent: June 14, 2003, 3:08 PM
To: Gaby
Subject: Good joke!

Dear Gaby,

Some joke. You should have seen the grin on Grandma's face. Blue's doing fine. We're all doing fine except no sister to help with the dishes!

I've been thinking I might go with Grandma to sheep

camp. I haven't asked her yet. Maybe I'll write her an email—ha ha! Grandma could use some help, at least during that first week, with getting things set up.

Today this white kid asked Grandma if she is a real Indian. Maybe that's another reason I want to go—to figure out what a real Indian is.

Yes, Blue's going to sheep camp. So stop worrying. Plus Grandma's old mare, Chaco, and the new pinto, Bandit. The pinto's small, barely 14 hands, with gorgeous markings and a sweet face, mostly white except for a black mask.

Blue will be strutting like a super dude, with two beautiful mares all to himself. Wait till he discovers there's a whole herd of ladies in the canyon!

Are any of the other recruits Navajo? Do the white ones call you names like "squaw" or "big chief"? Do you wish you could slug them?

Hey, sister, it's sort of ironic. You're an Indian inside the fort. In the movies the Indians are outside preparing to attack.

Here's a poem. That little kid at the trading post got me thinking.

When I was a child,
I didn't draw a line between my eyes,
down my nose, over my belly button.
One side Navajo,
one side white.
Now I have lines.
Who drew them?

You won't be hearing from us for a while. No internet in the canyon. No espresso either.

Take care of yourself, sister.

Stay safe, OK?

I love you.

Tess

I took a quick breath, hit "send."

I stared for a moment at the screen, then logged off. Grandma sat patiently, coffee cup empty, sort of staring into space.

Then Grandma stood up and already had a look that said, *Time to get on with business.*

"We need to get groceries. Final supplies for sheep camp."

"Mind if I come with you?" I blurted out my question.

"To the grocery store?"

"No, not the grocery store. I mean camp. Sheep camp."

Shimá looked at me, eyebrows furrowed. "Sheep camp?" Shimá kept staring at me. "You sure?"

"I can be in charge of Blue. Stay a week or two, help however I can."

"It's a long trail. And steep. Remember? It will take most of a day to herd the sheep down."

I stared at Grandma's green sneakers. "Gaby and I sort of talked about it." I didn't dare look up. I wasn't any good at lying. "We both thought it'd be a good idea."

Shimá nodded. "It'll be nice to have the company. I don't think the sheep'll mind."

Shimá smiled her teasing smile. I nodded. Nothing more was said.

I hadn't been down in the canyon since I was eight or nine and had tagged along with Gaby. She was always eager to go along, live in the hogan, and spend a couple of weeks with Grandma. I wondered how this year would be. Just Grandma and me. Maybe I had made a big mistake.

Shopping for groceries took a long time. Grandma double-checked prices for everything. We bought cans of baked beans, lard and flour for fry bread, a few sacks of onions, tinned milk, salt, sugar, black tea, and of course, ground coffee. All of it would get repacked at home and eventually loaded into the pickup truck. Gramps would drive the long way around to where the canyon opened up. From there he could drive up the riverbed all the way to camp as long as the riverbed was dry and we didn't get rain.

Grandma looked through our grocery bags and nodded. "I need a few things from Frank's Dry Goods. Want to come?"

"No, thanks." I didn't want to admit that everything in that store looked like old-lady stuff to me. "I'll wait in the truck, guard the beans."

"Suit yourself. I won't be long."

As soon as Grandma walked into Frank's, I scooted back to the café.

I signed into my email. Hit "new message."

Subject:
Missing you? Nope, too dorky.

From: Tess
Sent: June 14, 2003, 4:30 PM
To: Gaby
Subject: Sheep Camp

Hey, Gaby,

Sorry about those mean words I said when you were home.

I don't have another poem. Just thoughts that keep bouncing in my brain.

If only I could take back words,
the ones I wished I'd never said.
Or say
the words I didn't.

Do you ever feel like that?

Did a *Yé'ii* ever visit you in a dream? Should I worry about that?

I'm going to sheep camp.

Tess

P.S. Remember, you stay safe. I'll take care of Blue.

chapter twelve
sheep camp

Grandma led. She rode Chaco. Bandit followed close behind. It was the pinto's first trip into the canyon and her first time being surrounded by a moving, noisy herd of sheep and goats. Each time a sheep pushed past, Bandit leaped to the side, and my heart jumped up my throat. Loose rocks clattered down the cliff, scaring us both even more. The trail was often not much more than a wide ledge. One side went straight up and the other straight down. I tried not to look, since breakfast still sat like a stone in my stomach and threatened to reappear. Grandma kept talking to the young mare, coaxing her along. Finally

Bandit fell into a steady walk, keeping right behind Chaco, her nose practically in the old mare's tail. Blue and I brought up the rear. I led Blue and kept tight hold of his lead rope. He was not happy about being taken into unfamiliar territory. He kept tossing his head, trying to pull loose. I knew if he succeeded, he'd be out of this canyon in a flash and racing back home.

Grandma turned around, watched as I yanked on Blue's rope. "Relax, Tess. Talk to Blue. He's scared. Relax and Blue will do the same."

I tried to relax, tried thinking about all sorts of stuff: *How is my sister doing? Do I have it in me to become a real track star? Will I ever have a boyfriend, and will he be white or Indian? And why did I ever ask to come along to sheep camp?*

I thought about my grandmother sitting in the coffee shop, sipping a latte and sending an email. Today I suspected she had another surprise waiting for me. She wore a bright-orange backpack she'd bought—on sale—at Frank's. The pack bulged as if a basketball had been stuffed inside. I didn't ask. Grandma didn't explain.

A pile of loose rocks got kicked over the edge by a couple of goats. Blue startled, started pulling back, half-rearing, kicking.

"Ride him, Tess."

I shook my head. I was keeping my own two feet firmly on this narrow trail.

"A rider on his back will help him settle."

One glance over the canyon edge and again I shook my head.

"He'll learn." Grandma nodded. "You both will."

Up ahead the herd dogs, Shadow and Tag, kept the sheep moving, running back and forth behind them, nipping at their heels. The air was thick with dust. We were on the south wall of the canyon with no protection from the sun. It was hot.

"This next part is steep," Grandma cautioned. "Keep close to the inside."

The canyon wall was sheer rock and fell straight down several hundred feet. There was not a tree or an outcropping to break a fall. My stomach was now in my throat along with my heart, and with every tumble of loose rubble, it inched up higher. Now I remembered why I never liked hiking down into this canyon.

A raven had been following us, flying between the rocky outcrops, sometimes disappearing behind a canyon wall before reappearing. Its call sounded like water bubbling or someone gargling. I glanced at Grandma. She was watching it too.

Another hour slipped by, maybe two. The sun shone white-hot. Even the sheep seemed tired and mostly plodded along. The trail finally widened some, became not as scary. I kept a tight hold on Blue's lead rope, but now I could let my thoughts wander again: *How am I going to do long-distance runs on these rough paths? Where is my sister right now and what is she doing?* Suddenly Blue reached to snatch a mouthful of grass. His lead rope jerked. I remembered where I was, gave the rope a hard yank. "No snacking on the trail, Blue." He scrambled backward a few steps, tossed his head. The rope pulled right out of my hand.

Blue whinnied, ears flattened, and kept backing up,

trying to turn around. Another spill of rock tumbled over the edge, clattered down the cliff. I glanced at Grandma. She shouted in Navajo to Blue. I had no idea what she said, but the sound of her voice was clear. *Stop.* We both looked at the long trail we had just come down. No way was I going all the way back up chasing a dumb horse.

Show him who's boss. Mean what you say.

"Blue! Stop right there." I was more mad than scared. Just then Bandit nickered. Blue nickered back. Chaco joined in.

"Don't ever pull back like that again!" Blue heard me this time. He lowered his head. I grabbed the lead rope dangling from his halter. I looked at Shimá Sání, saw the smile on her face, and I smiled right back. I patted Blue along his neck, spoke softly, trying to sound like my sister. Blue gave me no more trouble the rest of the way down.

The trail finally leveled out and widened even more. We had almost reached the canyon floor. It was just a couple more miles to camp on level ground, soft sand, and with cottonwoods that would provide shade. We turned into a smaller canyon and followed the dusty bed of a dried-up arroyo. A ways ahead were wide patches of green. The animals picked up speed and trotted directly to what looked like a grassy meadow. Water trickled into this part of the arroyo from a series of springs. Puddles had formed in shallow muddy basins. I laughed. Baaing and bleating, the sheep and goats pushed and shoved like a bunch of schoolkids in front of an ice-cream stand that was handing out free samples. They drank greedily, their heads as close to the water as possible and their rumps sticking out to keep others from squeezing in. Betty-Boobsy was center front.

Grandma signaled to the dogs to keep circling the herd so they wouldn't wander. She dismounted and led Chaco to a big cedar with thick wide branches. The shade underneath was dark and cool. She broke off green needles and breathed in the spicy smell.

"For protection," she reminded me, looking around. "We're more than halfway."

The animals drank their fill and began grazing. Grandma signaled to the dogs that it was time to rest. The dogs didn't need a second call. They flopped down in the shade, tongues hanging out.

"Let the horses drink, then tie them under that clump of cottonwoods. See the two posts there? Keep Blue near the mares. It will help him stay calm. They're not in season yet. Once we get settled in camp, we'll have to keep Blue separated from the mares. Bandit's too young for foaling. Even if she wants to." Grandma's eyes were twinkling as she looked at me. "Even if she wants a little action."

"Grandma!"

Grandma smiled at my surprise. "Here in the canyon we tell it like it is—as you young people say." She smiled again and her eyes were laughing.

Grandma sat down on a long flat rock, watched as I tied the horses. She raised her eyebrows and thumped the bulge in her backpack.

"Delicious, for us." She chuckled at her secret joke and lifted out a round watermelon.

"Half for you. Half for me."

Suddenly I felt like I hadn't eaten for a week.

After a few minutes of slurping and swallowing, sweet red juice dripped off both our faces. Watermelon had never tasted so good.

Grandma handed me a water bottle. "Drink plenty." She spoke in Navajo. I looked at her, puzzled.

"In the canyon, no more English. Only Navajo. Don't worry, not much talking. Here we don't need many words."

"But Shimá, I've hardly spoken a word of Navajo all year."

"Your ears haven't forgotten and your mouth will remember."

"I've forgotten a lot since living in Flagstaff. How about some Navajo, some English?"

"Good, we meet on the bridge, half and half." She took a bite of melon, then looked at a boulder a few yards away. She spit a seed. Bull's-eye! "Your turn."

I slid a seed between my lips, aimed, spit. The seed fell a few inches from my feet. "Darn. I used to be a champion seed spitter. Better than Gaby. It made her so mad!"

"Practice," Grandma answered. "Everything takes practice."

Grandma tossed her rinds to Shadow, the older dog. Shadow caught it midair and then growled at Tag. I tossed mine to Tag. The dogs eyed each other, all the time growling and showing their teeth while chewing. After a few fast gulps, the rinds were gone.

Shimá slipped her knife back into its sheath and into her pack. "Time to go."

Something heavy landed on a branch overhead. We looked up. That same big raven perched right above us.

"He follows for a reason. Pay attention."

Pay attention to what? I wanted to ask.

"Ride Blue. The rest of the trail is easy but still a long ways."

"Ride? Still no thanks."

"Hop on Bandit behind me."

"I'm OK. I like walking." I wasn't about to ride like a little kid.

"Suit yourself."

She clicked for Bandit to giddyup. I untied Blue. He was antsy, eager to get moving. So was I.

chapter thirteen
hoghan, hogan

The hogan sat tucked underneath an alcove on the canyon's south side. The rocky overhang provided shade during the hottest part of the day. The southern exposure provided warmth during the evenings. Opposite the hogan, across the wide, shallow wash and beyond another fifty yards or so, the north wall of the canyon rose straight up nearly a thousand feet.

Snug and simple, the hogan was beautiful. Grandma's father had built the eight-sided log structure years ago. Shimá had grown up in this canyon with her parents and seven siblings.

I followed my grandmother to the hogan's single low door. She paused, and then pushed aside the heavy blankets hung over the opening. Inside the hogan the air was cool and smelled of earth, wood, and smoke from woodstove fires. At first I couldn't see a thing. After a few moments, I could make out a couple of chairs, a rickety table, and a kerosene cookstove. Blankets wrapped in plastic hung from overhead beams. Wooden shelving went from floor to ceiling on each side. One shelf was stacked with tin plates and cups, pots and pans, iron skillets, and a dented coffeepot—the outside black, a plug of wood stuck in the lid where a knob had once been. Other shelves held assortments of canned goods and storage tins, each clearly labeled—sugar, salt, flour, and coffee. There was a row of plastic gallon jugs marked "Water," and outside, next to the doorway, red cans for gasoline. There was even a shelf of books. Darn, I wished I'd thought to bring a stack of comics. In the middle of the hogan was a squat iron stove for cooking and heating. Its black metal chimney snaked up to the smoke hole in the center of the roof.

"First we build a fire. We warm up our *hoghan* and make her happy." Grandma handed me an empty orange crate. "Fill it only half full. The firewood is behind the outhouse."

I stepped back outside. Grandma was still talking. But to whom? Me? I turned around. She was chatting in Navajo, and I realized she was talking to the hogan as if it were an old friend.

There were a lot of things I didn't know about my grandmother. A lot of things I didn't even know I didn't know.

I loaded the crate and carried it back. Shimá had opened up two narrow cots.

"Here, take these blankets outside. Throw them over the tree branches to air out while we still have sunlight." She also handed me a water jug. "We'll boil up coffee." Her eyes twinkled. "No espresso, but good strong stuff. Cowboy coffee for real Indians." She shook her head, laughing to herself. "Fill the jug from the spring upstream from the corrals. The best one is near the foot of the tallest cottonwood."

The spring was right where Grandma had described. The water was cold and clear. I washed my face, then cupped my hands and drank. I could hear Blue nickering from the corral. He was not happy. I called to him. "OK, OK! Hold your horses!" Like Grandma, I laughed at my own joke.

I filled the jug and hurried back to the hogan. A thin line of smoke curled up from the chimney. Shimá stood in the doorway. She looked concerned.

"Blue wants out. Be careful with him." She took the water, motioned for me to sit down. "Once Blue claims this place as home, he can be let loose. The rest of our herd is somewhere in the canyon. Blue will find them." She smiled. "Never forget, Blue is a stallion, and for now we need to keep him in his own corral, away from the mares."

She poured water from the jug into the coffeepot. "Coffee will be ready soon. Then we eat and rest."

"Sounds great. I'll feed and water the horses."

It didn't take me long. Soon the horses were sniffing and sampling hay in their corral, and the sheep were grazing.

The dogs nipped at any sheep that acted like it thought the grass looked greener over the next hill. I was tired, thirsty, and hungry.

Shimá had spread a plastic red-checkered cloth over the two-person table. I unpacked the chicken sandwiches we'd made last night. That seemed like a century ago.

"Cowboy canyon espresso?" She laughed and poured two steaming cups. "Sorry, no latte." The coffee was black and muddy and tasted terrible, but the hot liquid soothed my dry throat.

"Thanks. Nice place, good service. Does this establishment offer free refills?" I smiled at my grandma.

Shimá smiled back. Her face had a warm, rosy glow. I wasn't sure if it was from the long ride in the sun, the warmth of the stove, or just because she felt happy. She refilled our cups. We sat slurping our coffee.

Gramps would drive the truck down next week and bring more supplies as long as the wash was passable, which it usually was until the July rains hit, monsoon season. The amount of rain that could fall during a monsoon storm could change the wash into a raging river, or so Dad had warned. Right now it was hard to imagine that the nearly dry bed could ever be more than a narrow trickle of meandering water. But the piles of rock and debris strewn high along the banks suggested that my dad knew what he was talking about.

I looked around the hogan more carefully. A few days ago Gramps had trucked in everything we needed. A dozen bales of hay for feeding the horses, canned food for us, and even his rifle, right above the door.

"Just in case," he had said when I rechecked my pack back at home. "Keep the rifle above the door, just in case."

"In case of what?"

"Both bear and mountain lion like the water in the canyon as much as anyone. But they aren't too fond of your grandma's coffee." Gramps was always slipping in a joke.

I washed up our cups in the basin. Grandma had gone outside. She had pulled out a couple of metal folding chairs from underneath a tarp and was sitting in the shade, looking out at the canyon's wide floor, nodding, smiling, and glancing at the sheep every few minutes.

"Is it OK if I go explore a bit?"

"Good idea."

I paused in the doorway. Blue was still prancing around the corral, nickering to the mares. "I'll take Blue. Maybe a walk will—"

"Not a good idea." Shimá looked doubtful. "If Blue gets loose, he doesn't know where home is yet."

"I'll keep a tight hold. We won't go far."

"You decide." Shimá handed me a water bottle. "Take water. Always. The canyon doesn't forgive mistakes. No second chances."

"Second chances?"

"Hot sun. Flash flood. Injury from thirst or drowning. No second chances."

I slipped the bottle into my day pack. "Thanks. I'll be back soon."

Chaco and Bandit were busy munching hay. The sheep had spread out along the wash, nibbling anything green. The dogs were stretched out in the shade of a cottonwood, tongues out, watching the herd. Blue was still prancing and dancing. He wanted out.

I snapped the lead rope back onto his halter and led

him down the wash, curious to see what I could remember from the last time I'd been here. For a few summers I'd come down to camp with Shimá and Gaby, stayed for a few days, and then gone back home with Gramps when he'd driven in with more supplies. I'm not sure why I hadn't come along the past few years. I guess a bunch of reasons. Mom switched to full-time at the hospital, Dad transferred to Phoenix, someone needed to help with chores at home, and I guess that was me. I had been glad to earn the extra allowance.

In the past, the best part of camp was hiking with my sister. I tried to help with the chores—stacking wood, hauling water—but it seemed I was more trouble than help. I remember climbing up the woodpile and the whole thing tumbling over. And when I hauled water, it seemed to jump right out of the bucket as I ran to keep up with my sister. It was more fun sitting in the shade by the spring and making mud pies or elaborate sand castles. The best time was when Gaby invited me to go to her secret waterfall canyon, even though getting there was a crazy, twisty, turning hike and the entrance was creepy dark, just a wide crack hidden in the curve of a side canyon. But it was worth being there, hanging with my sister, talking with her like a big kid. I'd never been in a canyon like that one. Gaby called it a slot canyon. At the very end was a deep round pool, sort of an oasis. The water was cool, clear, and the same deep blue as the sky. Water fell from a spring somewhere way up high, near the top of a sheer red wall, straight down into the pool. Gaby said the spirits were powerful there. She could feel them. If we sat very still, they would listen to our prayers.

The waterfall! I wanted to find it and put some sand

from that place into a special beaded pouch and send it to my sister. She would understand.

Blue trotted along behind me, content as long as I let him grab mouthfuls of grass and sniff at anything unusual. He looked all around, his ears twitching one way and then another. I guess that was his way of learning the trail. I stayed close to the riverbed. The canyon was more confusing than I remembered. There was no real trail, just a dry arroyo, and when it split in two, it was hard to tell which were side canyons and which was the main one.

Sometimes I'd see a rock formation I thought I recognized. Gaby and I had given names to some. "Knife Cut" was a rock wall split in two as if it had been sliced. "Pancakes" had flat sandstone slabs piled in a tall stack. "Sweet Slide" was a tall sand dune, smooth as silk. "That one's windblown," Gaby had explained. "That's why the sand's so fine, like sugar. And great for sliding down on a piece of cardboard."

I kept walking. Blue followed. The sun was already low over the western edge of the canyon. Sunset would come early down here. A gusty wind began blowing. I shivered. Blue started to whinny and sniff the air. *We should turn around and head back,* I thought. But darn, I wanted to find that waterfall canyon, at least the entrance. It couldn't be much farther.

Then I saw it, a narrow opening a little ways down the side of a pocket canyon. The wind whistled between these narrow canyon walls, swirling sand into dusty eddies, which made it even harder to see. Blue was not happy, but after the first few tugs, he followed. I had to pick my way around a bunch of boulders and barrel cactus before I could get to the opening. It was narrower than I remembered, just a few feet wide. Not wide enough for a horse to get through. Next to the entrance should be a big old cedar with twisted branches that looked like a spooky monster. Gaby had said that inside the tree lived a spirit that guarded the entrance. She always left two cookies as offerings. The tree spirit liked cookies, she always said—Oreo cookies. One was enough, but two were better. Sure enough, when we had hiked out, the cookies were gone. I had never suspected that my sister might have been the hungry spirit.

There was an old cedar and it was sort of near the entrance. Something about it didn't look right. Blue was doing his nervous prancing-around dance.

"Hold on, I just want to take a quick look." I tied him to the tree trunk and wished I had some cookies.

I took a few steps in. The air was stale and clammy, the silence just plain creepy. The waterfall would be at the end of this slot canyon, but I didn't smell or hear any sign of water. I hiked in a bit farther. A wall of debris from a rock slide stopped me. This wasn't right.

I hurried back. The sun had disappeared behind the canyon rim. Once I stepped out of the protective walls of that slot canyon, the wind hit like sandpaper. The air was murky with swirls of dirt and grit. Blue had scraped several holes in the ground, mad about being tied in a strange place.

"OK, Blue, time to head back. Shimá must be wondering where we are. Darn, I didn't want to make her worry."

Blue tried to trot past me. "You're going the wrong way, you stupid horse." I yanked on the halter rope. "I'm the boss. Behave!" His ears went back. He stepped on my foot. I smacked his rump. "Stop it!" I looked him straight on. "Settle down."

I started picking my way back to the main canyon. Nothing looked familiar. Our tracks were already covered with sand. The main wash was dust dry, which made it impossible to tell which direction was downstream or upstream. Walking downstream would take us farther from the hogan. "Come on, Blue, I think we go toward that finger-looking rock."

Blue stuck his nose in the air, snorted, and pulled back.

"Stop." I stared at the cliff walls. There wasn't much sunlight, and my eyes stung from the blowing grit. I wanted out of this canyon maze, out of the wind and swirling sand. But which way? Blue whinnied again, louder this time.

"You think you know the way?" I was so confused. And thirsty. Water. I pulled the water bottle out of my pack and drank the whole thing. That helped push back my panic. I'd been breathing way too fast and shallowly. *OK, calm down, think.*

I looked at Blue. "Gaby said you always know the way home. But do you know that the hogan is home now?" First day at sheep camp, and I had already messed up.

"Home, Blue." I tried to sound confident. "Home."

Blue led. I followed, holding on tight to his lead rope. It was nearly dark when I finally smelled the smoke coming from the hogan's woodstove. I put Blue in his corral, gave him a flick of hay, rubbed him down. I started up the path, my legs still a bit shaky, and stopped. I turned around and walked back to Blue. He trotted over and nickered.

"I owe you a big thanks." I reached over the top rail, rubbed him between his ears the way Gaby did. He bobbed his head, nickered again. "I know. You'd like a treat, maybe some sweet feed. I happen to have a pail of it under that tree."

I walked over, pried open the lid, and took out a handful. "How's this? No biting, understand?" Funny, I wasn't even worried. Blue scarfed up every grain and pushed at my arm. "Sorry, big fellow, that's it for tonight." I slid my hand along his silky neck and buried my face in his soft coat, smelled the sweet-and-sour scent of horse and sweat.

"Blue, maybe my sister was right. Maybe there is a big heart inside you." I gave him one more pat. "Tomorrow, Blue. If Grandma doesn't skin me alive first, tomorrow we'll find that waterfall."

chapter fourteen

dare to fly

But the next few days were busy with unpacking, sorting, hauling water, and herding sheep from pasture to pasture and back to the corral before nightfall. No time for even a short run. Finally, Grandma said, "Tomorrow is our day of rest. For you, a day of freedom."

"Will it be OK if I do some more exploring in the canyon?"

"Exploring is good." Shimá looked at me, eyebrows raised. "Getting lost is not."

I woke up in the middle of the night and couldn't get back to sleep. Something was bothering me. I listened hard for any strange sounds. The herd was restless. I heard the sound of their hooves on the hard rock in their corral and the songlike tinkling of Jack's throat bell. I walked outside, stared into the darkness. The mares stood side by side. Blue stood alone in his corral, staring straight at me. I walked over to him.

"Are you wondering where she is, why she hasn't come with a handful of sweet feed and a bridle to slip over your head? I miss her too, Blue." I rubbed between his ears the way Gaby did. Blue nickered back.

"Remember that wild ride in the dark with Gaby? I've never been so scared. Or so excited. It was like racing toward a finish line and passing everyone. Racing. No wonder Gaby didn't want to let go of you. I've never flown so fast, so smooth."

Blue bobbed his head as if he understood what I was saying. Made me laugh out loud.

"Teshina! Are you out there?"

I looked back toward the hogan. Shimá was standing in the doorway. "I'm out here, Shimá. I'm fine. Just needed to stretch my legs a bit."

I gave Blue one more rub. "Tomorrow's a free day, Blue. Might be a good day to find that waterfall, take a ride."

I headed back to the hogan, glanced back at Blue, and felt my heart leap a bit. "Maybe so."

I was up before sunrise. I carried in several loads of wood, gave the horses hay, watered the sheep, and mucked out all the corrals. Blue kept prancing back and forth, whinnying to me.

"I hear you! If I bring you along, do you promise to behave?"

Back at the hogan, Shimá handed me her orange backpack. "Your lunch: peanut butter sandwiches, Oreo cookies, two bottles of water. Drink one. Always have an extra."

"Thanks." I patted the zipped pocket of my vest. "I have another full bottle too."

She glanced at the corral. "If you take Blue, ride him. His reins are in the pack."

I squinted at my grandma, shook my head. "How'd you know?"

"Your face does its own talking." Shimá smiled a little. "Good for Blue. Good for you."

"I'm not sure I remember how. I've only ridden Blue once, sitting behind Gaby and holding on for dear life!"

Shimá chuckled. "Your butt remembers. You've ridden plenty of other horses."

"That was before Gaby's accident."

Shimá nodded toward the sky. "Keep an eye out for storm clouds. Rain up on the rim drains down into these canyons."

Shimá suddenly had a big grin on her face. "Remember, if you get wet, the fastest way to get home is on top of a galloping horse."

"Don't worry. I'm not interested in getting wet or going fast." I slipped on the backpack. "Thanks, Shimá. We won't be gone long. See you after lunch."

I snapped on Blue's lead rope, and we started down the wash. Last night I had dared myself to ride Blue. Today I would ride him.

Blue was eager. He hadn't been out of the corral for several days, and he tried to push right past me. I grabbed his halter, whacked his rump, and scolded, "Hold still. First we walk. Once you settle down, maybe we'll try something else." I swallowed. *Maybe. A walk or slow trot. Nothing faster.*

We stayed in the middle of the dry riverbed. The top layer of sand spread out smooth—like a page in a book full of stories but with no words. Footprints big and small crisscrossed the wash. Tiny tiptoe tracks made by stinkbugs, zigzag trails of lizards, and even a few slithering curves, probably the meandering tracks of a bull snake. Rattlers mostly stayed on top of the mesa.

I followed coyote paw prints to a clear, still pool, which looked like a polished liquid mirror hidden below an overhanging ledge. A dribble of water oozed from between two layers of rock, hardly disturbing the surface. I dipped my fingers into the pool—cool and wet—then splashed my face. Something bumped my shoulder. I turned, looked up, and laughed. Blue pushed me out of the way and stuck his nose into the pool. He sucked up the water like a kid slurping soda pop. I let him drink his fill while I sat on a boulder, closed my eyes, and listened to the wind whistle between slices of rock. My eyes blinked open, and I slowly looked all around. In the distance, a swirling dust devil danced up the slope of a sand dune like a miniature tornado. Salmon-orange sandstone surrounded us. This was the part of the canyon I now loved—the sheer walls, the silence, the immensity.

Up above was home, the mesa, where I could see from horizon to horizon and the world that expanded all the way to Flagstaff, to shopping malls, cell phones, running water . . . and school. I dreaded going back there in the fall, sitting by myself in the cafeteria, kids walking past me in the hall, no real friends. But maybe next year would be better; at least I wouldn't be one of the new kids. But I'd still be a Rez kid.

We walked on. I led, Blue followed. The canyon narrowed and eventually opened up. Now nothing looked familiar. The sun was straight overhead and hot. A few clouds had begun to pile up along the northern rim. A slight breeze began to blow. The air moving across my face felt great.

A swoosh of wings overhead broke the silence. I looked up.

CRAAWK!

"*Craawk* to you! I'm looking for a waterfall. Lead us to it, if you're so smart."

The raven landed on a branch and stared, its head cocked first at one angle, then another. Its mouth was wide open. Shimá said that's how these birds cooled off, but it sure gave the raven a spooky expression.

I ignored the bird. "Come on, Blue. Somehow we've got to find that side canyon." I started walking, hurrying now. Blue was tossing his head, pulling back. I knew he wanted to head home. The wind had turned cold, and goose bumps covered my arms. I hadn't thought about bringing a jacket.

A few drops of rain splattered on the sand. I shivered as the breeze turned even colder and gusty. The clouds were darker now, but moving away to the south. A distant rumble of thunder made Blue prick up his ears. More raindrops fell, slowly at first, then faster. Each drop left a wide wet splat on the sand. As quickly as the rain had started, it stopped. The clouds moved on.

Blue snorted, pulled back hard, and refused to move.

"Settle down. That's enough!" I meant business. Blue could tell. But he didn't budge.

One huge thundercloud rumbled overhead, blocking out the sun. A sudden pelting of rain and hail hammered down. Then nothing again. Wind rattled the leaves of the cottonwoods, swirled up a funnel of sand. Streaks of lightning flashed overhead. Cracks of thunder echoed between the canyon walls. A gray wall of rain rumbled closer and closer.

"I give up. I guess these storm clouds are for real." I looked at Blue. "Time to head home."

Blue pawed the ground. More lightning, nearly overhead, then a long loud rumble. Rain poured down as if the sky had split open. I was cold and soaking wet.

The fastest way to get home is on top of a galloping horse. I did want to get home, fast. So did Blue. I breathed in. I was scared. My insides were trembling, but darn it, I wasn't going to waste the day completely. No luck finding the waterfall—not yet—but I was going to ride Blue.

"OK, soldier sister, wish me luck!"

chapter fifteen

flying

I slipped the reins over Blue's head. He didn't flinch. He didn't fight the bit. I remembered how Gaby always talked to Blue when she was getting ready to ride. But I couldn't think of anything special to say.

"OK, whoa now, steady there, Blue." I climbed onto a boulder, wrapped the reins around one hand, and then grabbed hold of Blue's mane. I slipped one leg over his back, pulled myself up, and sat. Cold rain pelted down, mixed with sleet and hail. Blue's warm back felt good. I looked down, and the ground seemed very far away. My hands were shaking. I started talking to Blue, to myself, to nobody. "Anyway, what's the worst thing that could happen? I'll fall off?"

I stroked Blue's neck, patted his shoulders, kept repeating, "We can do this." He nickered softly, as if replying, *Of course. What's your worry?* I clicked my tongue, squeezed both knees, and pushed him forward. "Come on, Blue. Let's get home before we're in big trouble again."

Blue started walking.

I squeezed harder. "Over to the wash—we're going to take it nice and easy and trot back. Nice and *slow*, understand?"

Once Blue started moving, he didn't want to stop. I held the reins tight. He stayed at a trot, but a fast one. He tried speeding into a lope. I pulled him back. "Slow down. This is not a race."

Blue tossed his head from side to side. He knew we were heading home. How many times had my sister come racing back to the corral, face flushed, with a big grin? *Man, does he love to run, Tess—like flying.*

Like flying? Like that night we rode double in the dark?

"OK, Blue, OK, a little faster." I loosened the reins and let Blue switch to a steady lope. That felt better: a steady three-beat rhythm rather than his bone-jarring trot. Nice and relaxed, loping, maybe a gallop.

The rain was pouring so hard now I could barely see. Blue didn't seem to notice. He kept up a steady rhythm, legs reaching, hooves clattering against the hard wet rock and thumping across wet sand. Sometimes I got jerked to one side when he stumbled or slipped, but I pulled myself back to center as fast as he regained his rhythm. And then it really did seem as if we were flying. I loosened the reins even more, hollered to the wind, laughing, and before I had time to get scared, Blue sped up even more. He loved it!

"OK, Gaby!" I yelled to the cliffs, and the words echoed back. "Watch this!"

Watch this.

I whacked Blue's rump and hollered, "Let's go!"

Blue leaped forward like a spring let loose. His legs reached out, curled up, reached again, still faster, heedless of the pell-mell course straight up the wash. I put my head down against his neck, grabbed a fistful of mane, and held on tight. I could hear my sister's voice: *Feel the motion. Follow his rhythm. Look forward, lead him with your eyes.* I felt him reach, tuck, reach. I relaxed into this wild new rhythm, moved with it. Galloping, galloping. The world was streaking past. Blue's ears were back, his head forward. He was a flow of motion. I didn't care about the rain, the cold. We were flying! And I wanted to keep on flying all the way home.

Abruptly I realized we were nearly there. So fast. I wanted to keep going, but I realized that Blue was spent. His sides were heaving, his mouth foamy. I pulled back on the reins, although I didn't really need to. Blue slowed to a trot and headed straight to his corral.

Slow down, slow down, trot, trot, trot, walk. Walking home. Safe. Home.

My hands still gripped Blue's mane. We were both trembling. I could feel his heart pounding: *boom-BOOM, boom-BOOM.*

"We did it. Blue. We did it."
Ride Blue.
I did, Gaby. I did!
Soldier sister, it's your turn.
Stay safe. Fly home.

chapter sixteen
rain

Rain continued falling for days, steady, nonstop. Storm clouds kept piling up and moving over the canyon. Slanting rain blurred the horizon. Heavy drops thumped and pinged on the hogan's roof.

Shimá looked at the riverbed, already a wide muddy stream. "No supply truck this week."

She held out her hand. Raindrops splashed gently, slowly, but continuously onto her open palm. "A good rain, a female rain. Soaking the earth. Good for the corn."

"And good for running, nice and cool."

"Or fixing fences if we had those new rails Gramps was bringing." Shimá frowned. "Blue's corral fence needs repair before he figures out that with one big kick, over he goes, free to go courting."

"But we brought Blue here for breeding."

"For your mom's herd, not for these two, remember? Bandit's too young, and Chaco's too old." Shimá smiled. "Like us."

"Oh, Grandma!" I shook my head, laughing. "Maybe I'll take Blue for a short ride. Settle him down."

"Not until the rain stops. Too dangerous."

She gave me a stern look. "Trails down near the wash are soaked. Some places will be quicksand, not deep but dangerous for livestock or horses. The sheep will stay in their corral. The horses will too." She pulled a chair closer to the warm stove and sat down.

The kerosene lantern hung from the ceiling and gave a flickering glow to our little world. We slurped hot coffee. Shimá worked on a Sudoku puzzle while I wrote in my journal. I got bored and starting pacing. Then I remembered the books on the back shelf.

"What's this?" I blew off a layer of dust. "Emily Dickinson?"

"Yes. An old friend. Once I could recite many of her poems. Maybe you can read one for me?"

I looked through the book and found one Grandma had marked. I read it out loud.

Because I could not stop for Death,
He kindly stopped for me;
The carriage held but just ourselves
And Immortality.

At the end Shimá Sání's voice joined mine, and we finished the last stanza together.

Since then 'tis centuries; but each
Feels shorter than the day
I first surmised the horses' heads
Were toward eternity.

"Thank you, Tess. A good poem. When I was in school, I thought, I am Navajo, I should not read that poem. It was written by a white woman. She could speak of death. We do not. But I read and reread that poem." Shimá reached for the book. "Do you sometimes feel like that?"

"Like what?"

"The Navajo and white fight inside you?"

I nodded. "Because I go to school in Flagstaff, the kids on the Rez call me an apple: red on the outside, white in the middle. Rotten to the core. At school, the white kids call me 'Indian princess, heap-big squaw.' I don't fit in with either group."

"But you are both."

"Maybe. Was it like that when you went to school?"

Shimá Sání poked a couple more logs into the stove's fire. "School?" She shook her head. "Boarding school? I hated it. They cut our hair, burned our clothes, beat us if we got caught speaking Navajo. I swore to myself: 'I will escape this place and never speak English again.' I walked all the way home, over a hundred miles, proud but angry, and without a diploma. I didn't care. But my parents did. They cared about all that anger inside me and arranged a Blessing Way ceremony." Shimá looked at me. "The medicine man greeted me in English."

"English?"

"I said, 'I speak Navajo.'" Shimá shook her head. "Oh, I was so angry!" She wore a funny kind of smile.

"He said, 'Your Navajo and English fight. This ceremony is to bring them together, in harmony. Both can walk with you in beauty. *Hózhǫ́.*'"

Shimá paused. For a moment she sat slowly nodding. "At the end of that all-night ceremony, we went outside to greet the sunrise. The medicine man stood next to me. He shook my hand and repeated the closing prayer, first in Navajo and then in English. 'In beauty I walk. With beauty before me I walk. *Hózhǫ́ náhásdlíí'.* It has become beauty again.'" Shimá paused again. "I thought about what that medicine man said and realized I could learn from both languages, from both the speaking and the listening."

"I don't know which parts are really me."

"We all have many parts, Tess. We walk many paths, wear different shoes. Sometimes moccasins, sometimes sneakers. Some paths cross, some come together."

"But if I follow one path and leave the other behind, will I lose one? Will I get lost? Being at school in Flagstaff is taking one path. How do I make it cross with my Rez path? The two are so different."

"That is your outside path." Then Shimá tapped her chest. "But inside what are we? Red, white, blue, green? Apples, oranges? Ask Lady Dickinson. She wrote about many things. About being nobody. Or did she mean everybody? You are nobody too. All of us. Navajo and white. And everybody. Each time I re-read this poem, I see something new. Like having a new pair of glasses. But it doesn't mean I stop seeing through my own eyes. Those I keep."

Shimá tapped on the book of poems. "That little girl from Boston—what was her name?"

"Becca, Megan's cousin." I frowned.

"She did not see me, Tess. She saw a real Indian grandma with real Indian jewelry. She did not see this woman who loves her sheep, her stubborn goats, and a strong hot latte, who reads Emily Dickinson and sends letters to Iraq on the internet. Becca's eyes did not see these things."

"Just like the kids at my school."

"And maybe just like you."

"What do you mean, Shimá?"

"When you were little and you looked at my goats, they all looked the same. Now you see each one. You learned. We can all learn."

"I never thought about it that way."

"None of us does at first. And then we meet a goat from the herd that butts our old ideas. Makes us put on new glasses."

"Oh, Shimá, you are the best old goat."

"You are learning, Tess, you are learning."

Rain kept on, off, and on again for nearly a week. I loved thinking about that flying ride on Blue. I wanted to try it again soon, before I lost my courage. But the rain was relentless. Each dip up along the canyon's rim became a plunging waterfall. The colors of the desert changed. Oranges deepened to reds. The bark of trees and bushes blackened. Everything green brightened. Every smell grew stronger—spicy sage, blooming cliff rose, even the needles of the pine and cedar. The biggest surprise of all was the toads. Every evening choruses of chirping spadefoot toads echoed. Grandma explained that they stayed buried in the sand, sometimes for years, until their homes became drenched. Quickly they then dug to the surface, sang, mated, laid eggs, and were done. A cycle of life completed in just a few days. A whole cycle of life, just like that. I wondered if Gaby had ever heard them singing.

Our days fell into a pleasant routine. Sometimes I became impatient to get out—just me and Blue—to look for the waterfall. But each day was full of chores, cooking, eating, and cleaning up, and the setting sun.

Each new day we woke up surrounded by dark, walked outside, watched the sky lighten with dawn, and greeted the Holy Ones. Thin layers of color and light appeared, sometimes gold, rusty red, and eventually a pale silver blue. Mornings were clear, but rain returned every afternoon.

I helped Shimá Sání feed the sheep, saying good morning to each one. We worked side by side.

I fed the horses: old Chaco, little Bandit, and Blue last. Corrals were raked clean. Wood for the stove was carried. Each day I changed into my running clothes.

I ran along a path high above the streambed, but I had to run slowly. The path was rough and the rock was slippery. In the afternoons between downpours, I lunged Blue around and around outside his corral. We were both antsy for a long run. But first the rain had to stop.

Each afternoon after Blue was rubbed down and given another flick of hay, I helped Shimá Sání build up the fire and start supper. We ate early and we ate simply: corn or mutton stew, sometimes Navajo tacos with fry bread and beans.

Shimá Sání looked through the supplies. "Getting low.

Soon we'll need fresh meat." She looked at me. I didn't say anything.

After supper was quiet time. Boil water for dishes. Clear the table. Clean up. Check the sheep and horses. Sometimes I read a little poetry out loud. Sometimes there was time to write. I had begun a new journal about this canyon, Blue, and all the questions I wanted to ask my sister. And I wrote about the new ways I was trying to see. Shimá had spoken about Becca. I thought about Megan. I always saw her as a rich white kid. I never really saw her for who she was. Never really saw any of the white kids at school.

Nighttime was best. If the sky had cleared, we sheep-camp ladies sat outside on a big old fallen cottonwood. We seldom spoke. Sometimes we saw a shooting star. If so, we'd glance at each other and smile. Then nod. Each of us making a wish.

Sometimes the only sounds were the murmuring of the stream and the intermittent chorus of toads. Other times the night air was busy, alive with sheep bleating, horses nickering, rocks tumbling down, rattling against one another. Every once in a while, the wind whistled through the cottonwoods, and branches scraped against one another, making soft sighs or spooky moans. When a coyote howled, I listened for *yip-yip-yipping* replies from somewhere in the distant dark.

One night when the sky was especially clear, I stayed up later than usual. I sat alone and watched the darkness creep closer. Watched it deepen. I thought about Mom working at the hospital and Dad in Phoenix, and about kids at school. No one there really knew me. But I didn't know them either. They saw Indian, but when I looked at them, what did I see? I never really looked. Maybe it didn't need to be that way.

Maybe what the medicine man at Grandma's ceremony had said was true: the parts didn't have to keep fighting. I knew about sheep camp, about being in the belly of the canyon. About reading poems with my grandma. Comics with my sister. And I knew about racing with my team at school. Racing across the mesa. Running in sneakers, bare feet, or moccasins.

Right now, this moment, this night, here felt good. I was me—not part white, part Navajo—just me, sitting quietly in the night. The Milky Way was a river of stars—millions of universes.

Who's out there looking at us? Maybe they don't see red or white. What about Gaby and her desert nights? Are they quiet and dark? Or are her nights shattered with explosions and blasts that might mean who knows what? I shuddered.

Gaby, you were right. Blue is beautiful to ride. And something about him is wonderfully wild, scary and wild. But it's beautiful to feel, to know.

I wished on a star. *Be safe, Gaby. Please be safe.*

chapter seventeen
waterfall

The rains finally stopped.

The morning started out looking like trouble. The sky was a dull blue, and the air smelled strange. A thin line of milky clouds sat low and thick above the canyon rim. Not clouds, really, more like a dirty haze. Smoke? Maybe a fire near Flagstaff or the Grand Canyon, probably a controlled burn. Nothing to worry about down here. Rain—too little or too much—was the big worry here.

Blue pranced back and forth in his corral, kicking up dirt. Every few minutes he stopped, lifted his nose, and trumpeted. His whole neck vibrated, and his loud squeal swirled around camp like an invisible dust devil. Something wasn't right. Maybe he just needed to get out and run. The sheep were bleating and baaing as they milled around in their pen. Shimá Sání stood outside, watched Blue pace, and looked at me. "Go. Take Blue out. Run him hard."

"Now? Before I help feed the sheep?"

"I'm herding them upstream this morning to a high meadow. The ground there will be dried out enough to be safe. After so many days of rain, the grass will be tall and sweet." She glanced back at the corral. "Something has Blue all stirred up. Maybe the smell of that smoke, but maybe the smell of the wild mares. With water running in this riverbed, your mom's herd might be grazing near."

I fidgeted with a piece of baling twine I'd pulled loose from the hay. I was anxious to get going.

Shimá frowned as if she wasn't sure I was paying attention. "We've had a lot of rain, Tess. Unusual for this time of the year. Remember, it gives life and takes it. Water in some of the side canyons might be running high."

I nodded to Shimá and then hurried over to Blue's corral. I'd been hoping to get away early so Blue and I would have plenty of time to find the waterfall. This was my chance to get that handful of sand to send to Gaby. Being at the waterfall with my sister had felt sort of like being in our very own Neverland. Sometimes I swam in the pool while Gaby sat in the sand, quiet, not talking. The last time we were there together, we had written down our secret wishes, put them in a metal box that had a real lock and key, and buried it next to the pool. We had promised not to open the box until we each found our true love. That had been Gaby's idea. I hadn't said anything, but I wasn't sure I even wanted a true love. Today I would find that waterfall, for her, for us.

"Come on, Blue. We've got the whole day. Plenty of time to have our own adventure." I was pleased that the sound of my voice seemed to settle him down. I slipped on his halter, took my time brushing him, talking to him the whole time, waiting for Blue to relax before I snapped on the lead rope and led him out.

Shimá Sání was waiting in front of the hogan. She handed me her orange backpack. Every time I saw that glowing backpack and Shimá's pleased face, I had to smile. What a color. Today it didn't bulge with a watermelon. *Darn, that would have tasted delicious.* I slipped in the two water bottles I had filled at the spring.

Shimá nodded. "You are learning. Good, plenty of water." She pointed to the backpack. "And plenty of cookies."

"Thanks, Shimá."

"Today I'll take the sheep upriver and let them graze extra long. They're hungry for grass. Watch out for quicksand near the main wash. Blue has enough mustang blood in him to know to stay on firm ground, but . . . be careful."

"You be careful too."

"Give Blue a good run. He needs it." Shimá nodded. "You do too."

As we walked downstream, the wash grew wider and more shallow. I was sure the waterfall canyon was in this direction, but I couldn't remember how far. Shimá Sání was right—Blue was full of it. Wound up like a spring, prancing instead of walking. He sometimes shied, hop-stepping suddenly if a rock tumbled or a branch blew across the path. I thought about being on his back, loosening the reins and letting him run. What a wonderful terror it had been flying through the rain. No. I wasn't ready to ride him today, not quite yet. The weird-looking sky made me jumpy too. Besides, I needed to watch out for quicksand and the side canyon that would lead to the waterfall.

Nearly an hour went by. I didn't think Gaby and I had hiked this far from camp. But I had never paid much attention, since I always followed wherever Gaby led, busy with the guessing games she made up. Or we argued about some silly thing, maybe whether washing dishes was harder than drying, or whether folding clothes was worse than putting them away. We never decided which was stinkier: sheep poop or horse poop.

The wind had shifted from cool and breezy to hot and gusty, but the sky had cleared. If I could find the entrance to that side canyon, we'd have plenty of time to get to the waterfall and back before Shimá would start worrying. I remembered that once I got inside that narrow slot canyon, it was just a short way to the waterfall.

I was hot and already thirsty and hungry. Blue kept snatching at clumps of grass. Maybe we should take a break. I started looking for an overhang or alcove that would offer some shade.

Then I saw it: the giant cedar, old, with thick, twisted branches. "Blue, that's it! That's the entrance!"

Rocks and assorted debris had washed out of the canyon's mouth and formed a high mound that partly hid the narrow entrance. The entrance was hardly more than a wide slot, as if a giant had made a cut through the wall of rock. I recognized one enormous boulder, bigger than a car. Gaby and I had climbed it, had stood on its slanted, slippery top, holding our hands up high like victorious conquerors, shouting to the cliffs, "Hail, royal queens of the universe!" Of course, she was the real queen, and I was only the princess.

I scrambled up the boulder's side, slipped off Shimá's pack. Blue sniffed it. "Let's see what Shimá packed for us." Being here was special, sitting in this same place, munching a sandwich and a few Oreos. Gaby would break open a cookie and give me the half with the sweet filling. She didn't like that white stuff. I did. I'd make a trail through the layer of sugar with my teeth, then pop the whole thing into my mouth.

I counted the remaining cookies. Six. "I'll leave two as my offering to the tree spirit and eat the rest at the waterfall." I peered into the pack. "Here are your reins. Probably a good idea to slip these on now so I have better control. It might get spooky in there."

I had no problem sliding the bit into Blue's mouth. I buckled the reins and glanced at the sky. No change—clear and nearly cloudless, almost turquoise.

"OK, Blue, this is it. Waterfall or bust."

We squeezed through the entrance, barely. Blue snorted and pulled back. He didn't like going into such a narrow place. "I know what Shimá said about water in the side canyons, but it's OK. We'll be back out in no time." I felt closed in too, as if I were walking into some weird trap. Part of me wanted to turn around. I never really liked being in narrow places, and slot canyons were the worst. At least this one was wide enough for both Blue and me to fit through. But the sides rose straight up as if sliced by a giant knife. I clicked my tongue and snapped the reins. Blue took a few steps forward. "Good boy." I took a deep breath and patted his neck.

The canyon curved one way and then the other. For a while it narrowed to only a few yards across, but eventually it widened and became a large room, almost a cave, wide at the bottom, the opening at the top just a narrow slit. Only a crack of sunlight made it through. Now I was sure this was the waterfall canyon. I remembered how creepy this part felt and smelled—like a dark, stinky cave. The floor was covered in rubble—loose rocks and boulders with shallow pits of stagnant water. Blue stopped. I didn't blame him. The sheer sides felt too close, sort of suffocating. The air smelled rotten.

"It's OK, Blue. Just follow me." I tried to sound confident. I wrapped the ends of the reins around my hand so I'd have a firmer grip. I listened for the sound of water. Nothing. I remembered how the canyon narrowed one more time before it opened into the sunlight. And there up on the cliff would be our waterfall.

"*Craawk!*"

Startled, I looked up. Nothing. And I couldn't see blue sky through the crack anymore. Only clouds. Dark clouds. Lots of them.

My heart skipped a beat. How could the sky have changed so fast? Why hadn't I noticed? We should get out of here.

"But we're so close. Five more minutes max, I'm sure. Then we'll turn around, Blue. I promise."

Blue snorted, tossed his head, and began backing up. I pulled hard on the reins. "I'm not quitting now." A cold, wet wind, strong and stinging, whooshed through the canyon, stirring up swirls of dead leaves and dust.

Blue jerked back.

"A little farther, Blue. I hear something; I think I even smell it. Water or wet earth, maybe that little pond at the bottom of the waterfall. Come on."

We must be close.

Then something weird happened, something that felt like thunder, vibrations with no sound, as if the thunder were rolling through the ground beneath us. Blue threw his head back, and his front hooves pawed his protest, kicking up gravel.

"Stop it." I yanked hard. Blue pranced backward, kept stepping back. Then I heard it. Water! The roar of water. Boulders grinding against boulders. A wall of water was rushing down this canyon. Rushing right toward us.

I had been so stupid. I had ignored the warnings: Blue's protests, the low clouds, the blast of cold air pushed by a wall of water. I looked for some way to get to higher ground. Maybe a ledge, tree roots, or a pile of boulders? We had to get out of here.

The ground shook beneath us, and the strange thundering grew louder, closer, like a hundred wildly beating drums. The crazed, cold wind tore at anything growing from a niche or crevice. Behind that wind was water.

Blue stood still, eyes wide, sides trembling. Suddenly he reared. The reins ripped loose from my hand. His hooves scraped, clattered against the canyon wall. He twisted himself around. My heart seemed to stop. Blue could make it out even if I couldn't.

"Run, Blue!" I screamed.

But Blue didn't move. He stood there trembling, waiting. Somehow I pulled myself onto his back. I wrapped my arms around his neck, buried my head in his mane, and screamed again, "Run, Blue!" This time he ran. We were racing. Racing toward the canyon's mouth. Racing to stay ahead of the crushing water. I was jerked from side to side as Blue leaped over a fallen log, the roar of angry water coming closer, rocks rolling over rocks, boulders crashing against boulders. The canyon walls pressed in. *Hold on. Hold on.*

Then we were out. Out! A slap of cold rain hit me in the face. We were lunging through pelting hail. Water rushed out of the canyon, swirling, flowing thick beneath us. Blue's legs churned, pedaled, splashed through the thick red rushing water. My face stayed pressed against him, my arms tight around his neck, nearly numb from holding on. Holding on.

Blue leaped from the stream's edge onto a wide rock slab. He trembled, nickered, struggled up the closest dune. With each step, his hooves sank into the rain-soaked sand. He pulled them out, took another step. Slowly we made it to the top, above the rushing stream, to safety.

Blue's sides heaved—his whole body heaved. We stood above the flow of water. I looked back. Thick mud bubbled out of the canyon's narrow mouth, struck the pile of debris, and spread out. Shimá's orange backpack, carried by the rushing muck, bounced from wave to wave, hit a boulder, and disappeared, sucked down into a spinning eddy.

Water swirled around the trunk of the cedar, rushed and splashed, spreading out over the wide shallow wash like an angry scar.

I rested my head on Blue's neck, wiped away the foam dripping from his mouth, and whispered, "You saved me, Blue. You saved me."

I cried silent, slow tears. Blue lifted his head, nickering, his throat quivering.

I listened as Blue's heartbeat slowed and no longer hammered through his neck veins.

I sat up, half-laughing, half-crying, and sang out, howling to the canyon walls, "Yaaah, yaaah, yah!" Howling my thanksgiving.

The roar of the water had already subsided. The rain had softened to a gentle drizzle.

That quickly, the storm had passed.

I clicked my tongue. "Home, Blue. Let's go home."

chapter eighteen
moccasins

Shimá stood in front of the hogan, her eyes shaded with her hand. She watched as we approached, mud-covered and bedraggled. How long had she been standing there, waiting for us?

"You and Blue are safe. Alive and safe. I am thankful." She pointed to Blue's corral. "Rub him down. Put a wool blanket on him for warmth. Give him extra hay. I'll wait for you by the sheep corral."

I brushed Blue, scrubbed off the red mud caked on his legs, sides, and underbelly, and then rubbed him until he was completely dry. I stared at the mud in clumps around us. I picked up a handful, rubbed it between my fingers. Dirt and sand. Sand from the waterfall. What had Shimá said? *Rain—it gives life and takes it.* I stuck the sand in my pocket. Later I would put it in the beaded pouch I had made. I scooped up a handful of sweet oats, waited as Blue snarfed up every grain. "Sometimes we do get second chances," I said to him. I covered Blue with a blanket. "Thanks again, Blue."

Grandma stood by the corral's gate. I walked toward her and saw tears glistening on her cheeks. Suddenly I was running into her arms, and there I collapsed, shaking. Shimá held me. She began chanting in Navajo, swaying back and forth ever so slowly.

"Shimá, Shimá, so much water, so much mud. I thought . . ."

"You are alive. I saw the storm clouds, saw how low and dark they were. I knew you were looking for your sister's canyon. I was afraid I had lost you."

Tears spilled down, and I remembered. "Your new backpack. I lost your backpack."

Laughter. Shimá was laughing. "Oh, my very favorite new backpack? Good!"

I laughed too, and suddenly I felt joy. Pure, wonderful joy. I stepped back, looked at my grandmother, and said, "Blue saved me. He saved us."

Shimá nodded. "We will thank the spirits. We will give our thanks." She pointed to one of the lambs in the corral. "That one. Catch her and bring her to me. We will celebrate and give thanks for life. Yes, for your life."

I knew what was coming next. But this time I wanted to help with everything, even the hard part. I was alive.

Blue had saved us. I caught the lamb, held her against my chest with her legs tucked under, and began talking to her like Gramps would have, rubbing her forehead and stroking her neck.

I sat down, held the lamb close, and kept talking while Grandma walked to the hogan to get the things needed for butchering. Talking also kept me from remembering the sounds of water roaring and Blue fighting to climb out of the sucking swirl.

"Tess, face the lamb toward Big Sheep Mountain, *Dibé Nitsaa.* We face that way, *Náhookǫsjigo*, toward the northern mountains, the home of our predators: the coyote, lion, and bear. We do not hate them. They take their share, and we take ours. We respect one another."

The lamb lay still against me without moving or squirming. Her warmth felt good, felt safe. I closed my eyes and heard the fluttering beat-beat of her heart. So many different kinds of heartbeats, drumbeats. Life and death. *Sometimes we do get second chances. Lady Dickinson, who holds the reins of the carriage horses?*

Grandma held out her knife. I took it from her. A shiver of cold swept through me. The knife fell, landed with a clank. The lamb jerked.

"No worries." Grandma took the lamb. "You will be my helper."

I pressed my hands over my eyes. The bright sunlight made everything—the whole day—feel strange, almost like it was too close.

By the time I looked again at Shimá, the lamb lay lifeless in her lap. The pail was full of foamy red blood.

Shimá had chosen a lamb from one of her prize Churro ewes, sheep with tough wool and lean bodies.

Yarn made from a Churro was strong. Their meat tasted sweet and mild because they had so little fat. But Churros were a challenge, Shimá said, because they found ways to escape the corral. They wandered, and they climbed up the steepest arroyos and refused to return. Sometimes the wild part in them won. Churros were her favorites.

"Tess, you can look away as I cut the meat."

"I'm OK now. I want to help."

Shimá Sání made a clean straight cut down the sternum and opened the lamb's chest. A thin layer of fat pushed out. "Fat coming out of Big Sheep Mountain," Shimá said, smiling. "The white fat reminds us of the clouds. When the clouds spread across the sky, rain is coming. Always we are praying for rain, watching for rain." She kept working the skin loose from the lamb's muscles. "When rain is plentiful, grass is plentiful. The sheep grow strong. Rain means survival." Shimá looked at me. "But it also means danger. And so we learn."

I looked down, embarrassed to have been so foolish.

Shimá paused, picked up several spruce needles, and rolled them between her fingers. She breathed in their spicy aroma and then held them under my nose. "We smell the green of the spruce and give thanks."

Shimá continued cutting with quick flashes of her knife. "Nothing is wasted, not even the hooves. They'll give a good taste to the stew."

Shimá opened the belly and removed a shawl of fat wrapped around the intestines. "As soft as any wool blanket. And already warm!" She chuckled and gave it to me. "Drape it over the tree branch, next to the hide, wet side out."

It was heavier than I expected, and it slipped out of my hands.

Shimá pointed to a bucket of water. "Wash it first. We all make mistakes. Only the Creator is perfect."

That night we feasted on lamb ribs and stew. I ate until my stomach hurt.

After dinner Shimá stood up. She rummaged through one of the supply boxes and took out two packages. She placed them on the table. "For you."

The first package was from Frank's Dry Goods. I thought about all the odds and ends sold there—pots and pans, flyswatters, fabric, Western clothes, calendars. This was a shoe box. I looked suspiciously at Shimá.

"Go ahead. Open it."

I did. "Sneakers?" Maybe she had given me the wrong box. "Lime-green Day-Glo sneakers? For me? Really?"

Shimá Sání's smile grew wider. "Brand-new, never been worn."

I didn't know what to say. I didn't want to hurt my grandmother's feelings, but I didn't want to wear glowing-green sneakers, not even in the canyon.

"Green is a handy color. You can always see your feet." Shimá sounded very serious. "So you always know where you are." Then she began laughing. "Tess, no worries! I bought them in my size. In case you don't like them."

"Your size? But my feet are way bigger than yours. . . ." Suddenly I got the joke. I grinned at my grandmother, whose whole face looked entirely happy and satisfied. "OK, you got me with this one."

"Yes, you are understanding Navajo. Laughter is healing." She pushed the second box toward me. "Now open this one."

The second package was tightly wrapped in brown paper, a grocery bag turned inside out. I reached inside the box, and my fingers touched something soft. Could it be? I looked.

"Moccasins!" I pulled them out and held them to my chest. "Navajo moccasins!" They were softer than anything I'd ever held, made of white doeskin with suede bottoms. I slipped them on and stood up. The soft leather wrapped up my legs, almost to my knees. They fit perfectly.

"Made for your *kinaaldá* ceremony. You are changing from girl to woman. It is almost time."

I gave my grandmother a long, big hug, very un-Navajo. She laughed. "All is beautiful again, *hózhǫ́*." Her eyes were smiling too. "Go outside. Take them for their first walk here, tonight, in this canyon."

I stepped outside, sat on a rock, and looked up at the immense sky. "Thank you for keeping us safe, Blue and me. Please keep my sister safe." I walked to the sheep corral, thanked them for sharing their friend. Then I went over to the horses. "All is beautiful again, *hózhǫ́ náhásdlį́į́'*." Blue nickered and nuzzled my hand. I laughed, remembering that time he bit me.

Flying on Blue. Gaby was right. I fingered the sand, still damp in my pocket.

chapter nineteen

wild

The warmth of the day had cooled to evening's chill. When I returned to the hogan, Shimá was already sleeping. I lay down on my cot, pulled up the wool blanket. As soon as my head hit the pillow, I was out. But not for long. I felt the earth trembling, and I was gasping for air, trying to shout, to run. My legs wouldn't move. A wall of water rushed closer. My eyes flew open. All was dark. I was in my bed, safe. The nightmare was gone. I curled up tight on the narrow cot, reached for floppy-headed Pluto, and remembered I hadn't brought him to sheep camp.

As soon as I closed my eyes, it started again—the same

nightmare, water roaring, the ground shaking. Blue rearing. Red mud swirling around us. In the distance was a giant boulder. A *Yé'ii* stood on top. His face was sad, and his empty hand was held out. Where were the cookies? Of course. They were gone. Everything. Washed away. Gone.

Now the *Yé'ii* was riding Blue away. Blue broke loose, whinnied. Stop. Come back. I tried to yell. No words came out.

I woke up, sweaty and shivering. Had something happened? To my sister? To Blue?

Another *Yé'ii* dream. *Yé'ii* weren't supposed to appear in dreams. Gaby had explained that to me a long time ago. I was little and hadn't really listened. She had said something about needing a ceremony if one ever did appear in a dream, but why? And what happened if I didn't tell anyone and never had a ceremony?

Blue whinnied from his corral, and this time it was real. I had never heard him call out in the night before.

I wrapped the blanket around me and hurried out to the corral. Blue sniffed at me, snorted, backed away, began running in circles.

"What's wrong? Another storm coming?" I searched the sky, but it was clear. The full moon shone silver on the canyon walls, changing the familiar landscape into an eerie place of stone statues and shadows. I listened but heard nothing unusual, not even a coyote yipping. Blue trotted over, tossed his head, blew out a snoutful of dust.

"Still upset about today?" I shivered. "Me too." I held out a flick of hay. Blue backed away. "Maybe we both need to take a long run, feel solid dry earth beneath us." I tossed the hay into the corral. "OK. First thing in the morning, we'll take a run." I filled his feed bucket with oats, glanced around one last time, and walked back to the hogan.

The next time I opened my eyes it was morning. The nightmare had not returned, and I could smell coffee.

Shimá stood in the doorway, staring at the horses.

Blue was prancing around and around in his corral, whinnying and kicking at the fence. I got up, hurried over to her. "What's going on with him?"

"The mares. He smells the young one. She's come into season. Earlier than I figured."

Blue snorted, ran from one end of his corral to the other. I threw on my clothes and started out the door. Shimá held my arm. "Stay here. He's a stallion, too crazy to go near when he's worked up like this."

Blue ran straight at the fence and reared, his front legs wheeling. The top railing splintered and tumbled off. Blue jumped over the remaining rails and tore right over to the mares. Already Chaco and Bandit were prancing, trotting, calling back. He kicked at their fence until the railings shattered and leaped into their corral. Tail up, ears back, he bit at their rumps, rounding them up. His own herd. He wanted them out.

"Stop, you stupid horse! Stop!" I yelled.

"Wait." Shimá held tight to my arm.

Blue raced around the mares, reared, and then jumped over the broken railings. The mares followed. Blue circled back, nipping, urging them on, and led them down the wash.

"I'm going after them."

"Stay here. Blue's dangerous. I need to move the sheep

upstream where they can graze. The dogs can guard them. We can go after the horses together."

"No, Shimá. That's too much for you, and it'll take too long. I can run after the horses right now. They're headed down the wash. Their tracks will be easy to follow."

"I don't know. . . ."

"Better if I go now. I'll catch the mares, bring them back."

"Stay away from Blue."

"Blue won't hurt me. I know he won't."

"Catch Chaco. Bandit will follow. Once they're back, Blue will show up." Shimá frowned. "One hour. Be back. With or without the horses."

I grabbed a halter, stuffed my pockets with sweet oats, and raced down the wash. After a half mile or so, their tracks left the main canyon and veered off into a muddy arroyo. I had gone that way once with Grandma and the sheep. A little farther down was an open area with a wide meadow. Maybe that's where Blue was taking the mares.

I couldn't see them, but I could hear them calling to one another. I wasn't sure which way to go, so I ran to the top of a low dune. There they were.

Blue was shiny with sweat, running around the other two, prancing, head bobbing, tail held high. Darting one way, then the other, he never stopped moving. He kept prancing around Bandit, nipping her rump, nickering, calling to her.

She began to return his dance.

Bandit high-stepped in circles with her tail arched. Bobbing her head, she answered, snorting and neighing an unmistakable reply.

Blue neighed too. They touched noses, sniffed.

Backed away, tails swishing, heads held high. Blue trumpeted. His entire throat vibrated. His body quivered.

Around and around he circled, ever closer, kicking up grit and dust.

Bandit pranced back, head raised, and screamed in a high, excited voice.

Their heads bobbed, and their eyes were wide and fixed on each other. The rhythm of their movements quickened until suddenly Bandit stopped. She stood statue still, panting, her back legs planted, slightly parted. Blue circled behind. I couldn't look away. I had watched plenty of livestock mate: sheep, goats, and cattle too. But it was never like this. This was powerful. Beautiful.

When they were finished, Bandit slipped from underneath Blue. Tail down, she walked over closer to Chaco and began grazing.

Blue trotted to the top of a nearby ledge and turned to look at me.

He watched as I approached, holding out a handful of sweet oats, calling his name. He hesitated, still looking at me. Suddenly he spun around and took off.

Blue was gone.

chapter twenty
broken

Chaco and Bandit were easy to catch. They weren't interested in anything but grazing now. I looped a lead rope around Chaco's neck and slipped on the halter. "Come on, we're heading home." Bandit trotted behind.

I put the mares in their corral. Shimá had tied a temporary board across the smashed fence. I got some wire, found a hammer and jar of nails, and pounded the board more firmly into the posts.

"Shimá?" I called, thinking she would be somewhere around.

No answer, and the herd was gone. Then I remembered. It would take Shimá an hour or more to get them to the nearest pasture and for her to return here. I still had time to catch Blue before Shimá got back. I ran back to the meadow and followed Blue's tracks.

I heard the birds before I saw them. A strange, loud hissing—ugly and unnerving. Only one kind of bird made such a disgusting and terrifying sound. Vultures! "No!" I yelled. I ran faster until I saw them. "Get out of here, you stupid birds!" I shouted, waving my arms. A dozen or more birds rose up out of the arroyo like a black cloud, circling high above, around and around, but never out of sight.

Blue's tracks were clearly visible in the damp sand. He had turned into a narrow, steep-sided arroyo, climbed out of the bottom, and followed a trail along the top. It was hard to climb up the sides of the arroyo. The sand was still loose from the recent rains, and it was probably forty or fifty feet to the top. Blue must have struggled too, since I could see that his hoofprints were sunk deep into the sand. "Blue! Where are you? Blue!"

Then I heard something. Something I wanted to hear. Blue?

I listened again. At first nothing. Then the softest sort of nicker.

I ran along the top edge of the embankment. My throat felt dry and tight, as if it were closing up. I followed Blue's tracks until they stopped. The entire side of the embankment had collapsed. I realized Blue's mistake. A few days ago this arroyo must have been swollen with water. The rushing torrent had undercut the steep sides, forming a cornice, a sort of ledge hanging out in space. Nothing underneath to support it. But from the top, it would have looked like solid ground.

Blue had run along this ridge. He had been standing here, where the tracks ended, when the lip of the earthen embankment collapsed. Blue was caught in the mud slide and tumbled straight down to the creek bed.

I looked down.

"Blue!" I screamed.

Blue whinnied. He tried to stand, his hind legs scraping against rock, trying to push up. The slabs of sandstone were streaked with blood. He tried again but fell back.

"Blue!" I ran, half-sliding, half-running down the slope of mud, rock, boulders, and broken branches "Blue!"

Blue raised his head. His front legs were twisted beneath him. Splintered bones stuck out of the torn muscle and skin.

I stopped, suddenly dizzy. I closed my eyes. This wasn't happening.

I crouched next to Blue, cradled his head. His neck was wet with sweat. I rubbed between his ears the way that Blue loved. I stared at his legs. What should I do? I knew the answer. I didn't want to know it.

"Shimá will know what to do. I'll get bandages. It'll be OK. It will. It will."

I wiped the froth from his mouth. "You need water."

I didn't have any water.

chapter twenty-one
sing

I tried to run. My legs were like wood. But I had to run.

Smoke curled up from the hogan's chimney, blue-gray smoke. Perfectly normal. Perfectly fine. Maybe I was waking up from another terrible nightmare. When I stepped inside, Shimá would offer me a cup of coffee. Blue would be waiting in the corral.

Shimá looked at me.

"Blue?" she asked.

Her one-word question, his name spoken, it hit like a blow to the stomach. "I found him." It was hard to breathe, hard to speak. "Blue's hurt."

"How bad?"

"His legs. His front legs." I looked down. "Broken."

Maybe the legs can heal. Maybe we can wrap Blue's legs and find a way to make them heal.

I looked at my grandmother. "What should I do?"

"*T'áado 'áhó'ne'ída*?" my grandmother answered me in Navajo. "What is there to do?"

"Tell me what to do."

My grandmother did not answer.

I already knew. There would be no healing, no second chance.

The answer would break my sister's heart.

"Tell me how to do it," I whispered.

"You know." She reached for the rifle over the door. "I will come with you."

"No."

She placed the rifle on the kitchen table. "I understand."

I walked outside, sat near the stream where the sand was cool and damp. *No, I cannot do this.* I closed my eyes and saw what I did not want to see. Gramps had cradled the young sheep and sung. *We sing as life comes into this world. We sing when life travels out.*

We sing.

The vultures would come back soon.

My mind filled with sounds and visions. I could hear Blue's nicker. I could feel the wind whipping through my hair, the river rushing beneath us. From the top of a cottonwood, a raven stared. A *Yé'ii* with a blue face sat next to it. He reached toward me, holding out his hand, asking. I had nothing to give, nothing. My sister had left. We had made promises. I hadn't been able to keep mine. Could she keep hers? *Will she ever forgive me?*

Blue whinnied. The raven hopped one branch closer. I shook my head, "No!" An eagle feather lay on top of my pillow. *Fly, my little sister.*

We did. Blue and I, in this canyon.

I opened my eyes. A lizard ran across the sand, its tongue flicking in and out. I looked back up. The tree was empty—no raven, no *Yé'ii.* No whinny from Blue.

I knew what I had to do. I knew I had to do it now.

chapter twenty-two
blue

I walked back to the hogan. Grandma stood in the doorway, tears in her eyes. I looked at the kitchen table, stared at Grandpa's rifle. Finally I picked it up. The cold metal felt strange in my hands.

I prayed. Shimá Sání stood next to me. Neither of us spoke. She took a pinch of corn pollen from the pouch she always wore and sprinkled it over the gun while quietly speaking Navajo.

I slipped Grandpa's ammo box into my pocket.

"Are you sure you want to go alone?"

"This is mine to do."

My grandmother handed me a plastic jug. "Water."

I was close, almost back to where Blue lay, when I saw them again, the ugliest birds in the desert. Red naked heads. Black thick bodies, hunched over. Turkey vultures. Those birds were so big they weighed down the branches where they sat, waiting. I picked up a rock and threw it. Then another and another. The vultures flew up, a swirl of feathers, their wings beating hard.

They circled, black against the hot white sky, shadows that glided in slow, wide circles, dipping lower with each turn. My heart hurt.

Blue could hardly lift his head. I sat down, put his head in my lap, held him, sang to him. I poured water into my cupped hands, but he would not drink. I held Blue until my arms were numb. I stroked his long powerful neck, dark with sweat. I closed my eyes, rocking, rocking, and as I stroked Blue's head, I sang. I had set the rifle behind his head. Blue would never see it.

Gently, so very gently, I placed his head in the soft sand.

I stood and picked up the rifle.

"Look, Blue, up there, turquoise sky, everywhere," I said softly.

Turquoise sky.

"Fly home," I sang.

"Fly home."

chapter twenty-three
stone

I carried rocks.

I carried rocks to cover Blue so the vultures could not reach him.

I carried rocks until every part of me hurt.

I became like stone.

I heard someone yelling, crying, singing.

"Aaaah-ya! Aaah-ya-ya, yah!"

It took a moment before I realized it was my voice, my tears, my song.

Then I was silent. *Run*. But I could not move.

Sorry does not lift a raven back into the sky. Run. Run. RUN.

Sorry does not give a second chance.

I tried to run but couldn't. I walked.

When I finally returned to the hogan, my grandmother took the rifle and put it back in its place above the door. I stared around the room. It looked just the same. How could that be?

"I covered him with rocks."

Shimá put a cold wet cloth on my forehead and wiped my face. "You did what needed to be done, what you never wanted to do. First, drink." She handed me a cup of water. "And then we must accept the journey. Often I have prayed for that acceptance. The second dawn at day's end, unto the blue skies, there's a beginning, and there's an ending—all in sacredness and beauty."

"I need to tell Gaby."

"She will know." Shimá gestured toward the wash. "Go. Walk with your sister." She continued speaking in Navajo, and I understood her words. "Tears feed the earth, become earth. Let the earth hold you."

I began to walk. Then I ran, and in the running, memories flowed through me.

Drums calling. Families walking in silence, a procession of people as they passed by two little children.

Two little children. Life walks forward.

Run. Run. Run.

My legs became a song.

Blue,
forgive me,

teach me.
Canyon walls,
hold me,
hold me.
Who will lift the raven out of the dirt?
How does the soul forgive itself?
I run to ask you,
forgive me.

I ran until there was no running left. I climbed to the top of a dune covered with ripples like frozen waves. The sky had changed to the deep purple-blue of just before sunset. Evening.

This day ending.

I sat in the warm sand, wrapped my arms around my legs, rested my head on my knees, and closed my eyes. I saw Blue bobbing his head, sniffing for sweet oats. I held out my hands. Blue nuzzled my hand and ate. He raised his head, trumpeted to the turquoise sky.

My tears fell onto the sand.

chapter twenty-four

email

No more rain, not a drop. Gramps arrived after a few days. The wash had dried out. It was back to being a wide, empty river with a trickle of water. He and Shimá had coffee while I unloaded the pickup. I knew what they were talking about.

"Need a lift back to town? I don't charge much."

"Sure. I need to send a couple of emails. Maybe I can get a return ticket for your next trip back?" I tried to smile.

"No problem."

"I'll get my things; won't take long."

I was stuffing a few clothes into my backpack when

Shimá came into the hogan. She walked over to the shelves on the back wall and slid out a book.

"Maybe you would like to borrow this?" She handed me the copy of Emily Dickinson's poetry.

I didn't know what to say or how to thank her for the book, for sheep camp, for everything. "I would like that." Then I let my un-Navajo self wrap my arms around her. "You going to be all right here alone?"

"This is my home."

"I'm coming back. I still have that waterfall to find."

"When you email Gabriella, tell her she was right." Shimá grinned. "Those sneakers didn't fit you, but they sure look snazzy on my feet. And she said lime green was your favorite color."

Gramps gave a short honk. He wanted to get back on top of the mesa before the weather changed or the wind kicked up.

"OK, OK," I called. "I just need to say a few good-byes."

Shimá looked puzzled.

"Yes, I might even miss those noisy sheep! And the mares." I smiled at Shimá. "Bandit might need a little extra hay soon."

Shimá raised her eyebrows as her reply.

And then we left. I sat next to Gramps in the front.

"Any word from Gaby?"

"Your sister emails your ma almost every day."

"She doing OK?"

"Seems to be."

After that, neither of us said another word the rest of the ride out of the canyon. That was the Navajo in me.

As soon as we got home, Mom and I drove to Tuba.

My hands were shaking as I touched the keyboard. There was email from Gaby.

From: Gaby
Sent: July 5, 2003, 5:04 PM
To: Tess
Subject: Everything OK?

Hey Little Sister,

Something's got me really worried. Something's happened, I can feel it. Are you OK? Write back—SOON.

Gaby

P.S. I miss you. My turn here for dish duty, and I've never seen so many!

I hit "reply." I stared at the screen. Finally I wrote.

From: Tess
Sent: July 8, 2003, 1:27 PM
To: Gaby
Subject: RE: Everything OK?

Gaby,

I'm OK. But you were right. Something terrible happened. Blue ran off and got hurt. In the canyon.

There was nothing we could do to save him. Forgive me, someday.

Tess

That wasn't anything like what I had planned to say. All my words had dried up. I hit "send" anyway.

Mom and I shopped for groceries. It felt like she was tiptoeing around me.

"Shimá asked me to get her more yarn. I'm going over to Frank's. Want to come along?"

I shook my head, smiling, wondering if Grandma was wearing her new sneakers. "I'll get some coffee. I already miss Shimá's cowboy brew. Meet me back at the café?"

Mom had that worried look of hers. "It's too soon for a reply."

I shrugged. "Maybe."

I logged on. There was a new message. From Gaby.

From: Gaby
Sent: July 8, 2003, 2:12 PM
To: Tess
Subject: RE: Everything OK?

Tess,

Maybe what's hardest of all is doing what we swore we would never do. And then we have to make a choice. That's one lesson Lori taught me.

Blue made his choice. He chose to run free. Maybe I knew all along that's where his heart was.

Forgive you? I cried with relief reading that you are all right. That's what I care about, Tess—family. Here, every day, families are blown apart.

The rest we'll figure out together.

I love you,
Gaby

twenty-five
łį́į' dootł'izhii, blue horse

Sometimes we do what we swore we would never do. The words kept echoing inside my head even though I didn't want to hear them.

It was time to bring supplies back down to the canyon. I asked Gramps if I could go along.

"Are you sure?" he asked.

"I am." I was afraid to see that empty corral. But I had promised Shimá that I'd be back.

The truck bumped over the last part of the road—two parallel lines of gray rubbery tire marks left on the long smooth slabs of bare red rock. The truck eased down stone inclines, inching our way lower and farther into the canyon. Heat radiated from the rock walls as if someone had turned on an oven. A scattering of juniper and pinions twisted upward. How did those trees grow out of the bare rock? Sleek lizards scurried from sunbathing perches and disappeared beneath boulders. Silence, except for us, rumbling, creaking, the truck's brakes squealing. The truck seemed no more eager to reach our destination than I was.

Grandpa and I didn't talk. We didn't exchange one word until we drove up the dry riverbed and bumped to a stop in front of the hogan.

"Ready?"

I knew Gramps was looking at me, worrying.

"Guess so."

He opened his door, got out. I opened mine.

Shimá Sání stood in the doorway of the hogan.

I had promised myself I would not cry. Promises. So easy to make. My hand reached into my pocket. It was still there, an unpolished hunk of turquoise. Gaby had sent it when she first got to Iraq. At first I didn't know why. Then I realized. It was for Blue.

Blue. Damn that horse.

Shimá Sání nodded her welcome. Familiar smells escaped from the hogan—coffee and mutton stew. Somehow she knew we were coming today.

"Got cowboy coffee. Looks like you need some."

I wiped dusty tears and my runny nose on my sleeve. "Thanks, I could use it." Shimá put a steaming mug into my hands. I looked at my grandma's face, really looked. Not a very Navajo thing to do. My hands stopped shaking. Shimá Sání. One fine lady.

"This place still give free refills?" I asked.

"Only for regular customers."

We both smiled. "It's good to be back."

Gramps handed his empty mug to Shimá. "Thanks. Best coffee around." He chuckled. "Time to start unloading. We brought down extra supplies, plus a dozen hay bales. That should last you for a few weeks in case the rains return."

"Need some help, Gramps?"

"I'll hand you the boxes of food. The hay is easy to toss next to the corral."

The corral. I did not want to look at the corral.

I carried in the boxes. Shimá unpacked. She paused, laughed softly. "Good, more Oreos." She glanced at me. I smiled back and touched the turquoise in my pocket. I knew. I would take Gaby's gift to the waterfall.

Grandpa stepped into the hogan. "My stomach says it's time to eat. My nose says this is the place."

Shimá nodded for him to sit down. "Teshina, how about you?"

"No, thanks. There's something I need to do first."

I stepped out of the hogan. I dared myself to look, to see the corral.

There was no one prancing in circles to greet me.

No familiar nicker. No impatient snorting.

No Blue. Not today. Not ever.

I held on to the fence rail.

Blue, you chose wild. I wanted you to choose me.

I closed my eyes, swallowed, let the tears fall.

Łį́į́' Dootł'izhii. Blue Horse. Fly home.

I was ready for that refill of cowboy coffee.

twenty-six

ghąąjį’, october

Summer stops. Autumn begins. Winter soon walks forward. *Ghąąjį’*. Season of change. The morning sky was bumpy with clouds. Fall had arrived.

I sat at the kitchen table and finished writing a letter to Gaby. Sometimes I preferred actual letters. A letter can be held, carried in a pocket, and reread anyplace. Sometimes I needed to touch the words, smell the paper.

Gaby preferred email. She could type almost as fast as she could talk. She always had lots to say. Every Friday on the trip home from school in Flagstaff we stopped at the espresso café in Tuba City. Yesterday there were emails waiting for Shimá, for Mom, and one for me. She always wrote something about Blue. I was glad for that.

From: Gaby
Sent: October 25, 2003, 7:01 PM
To: Tess
Subject: Thinking . . .

Tess,

I've been doing a lot of thinking. I still miss Blue, every day. But you did right. Sometimes I wish I could rewind time and maybe make different choices. When I think about coming home and walking down to Blue's corral, it's hard, Tess. But it's not about forgiving you—it's about forgiving how life is. If I die here tomorrow, you'll be madder than hell at me. Sometimes there's no real understanding—just accepting the choices we make, accepting what happens.

I guess my talking about death isn't very Navajo, but I'm half white too, just like you. And guess I'm still trying to figure it out. Life. And death. Even mine.

Be safe, little sister, my soldier sister. I love you.

Gaby

Last week Gramps had phoned me at school and asked, "Will you ride with me? On Veterans Day?"

"Ride? I don't have a horse."

"Your mother said you could ride hers."

"I'm out of shape for long-distance riding. The last time I was on a horse was in the canyon." My throat tightened up. I swallowed.

He asked again. "On Veterans Day. I'd like you to come home and ride with me."

Gramps waited to hear my answer.

"Let me think about it."

Across the Navajo Nation, schools were closed on Veterans Day. My school in Flagstaff wasn't closed. What would I say to my coach, to my teachers? Then I realized the white part of me in Flagstaff and the Navajo part of me in Tuba City didn't need to fight. My Navajo voice was ready to say at my white school: *My sister is a soldier, carries a rifle, and is willing to die for her country. I am Navajo, and I want to honor her and all our warriors.* At first it was scary to say those words out loud, to explain to teachers and kids that for Navajo, honoring warriors is serious, almost sacred. But then it felt good.

I came home.

Veterans Day. Everyone has a part, helping or riding. Families prepare all week.

Veterans groom their horses so even the hooves shine. Soldiers from any war or conflict—both women and men—clean and polish tack, get uniforms out, and prepare to ride.

Before sunrise I fed the horses that would stay behind, old Chaco and Bandit. Extra hay for Bandit now, her sides already a little swollen. *Good job, Blue. When Gaby comes home, a little foal—a part of Blue—will be here to greet her.* Maybe it'd be a colt, a beauty like Blue.

I stood outside and looked across the mesa. It was still dark, but lights were on in most of the homes and hogans. Soon at each ranch, including ours, riders would mount their horses. Off they'd go, riding across the washes and arroyos, over sand dunes and rocky red paths, toward the chapter house, the official governing and gathering place of each community. Along the roads, families would be waiting and watching, eager to be the first to spot a horse and rider. Kids would put up hand-printed signs: *Free coffee and doughnuts for veterans.*

Gramps walked up to me. "Ready?" He handed me his US Marine Corps cap, the kind that folded flat so a soldier could tuck it into his belt. "Would you like to carry this?" He hesitated. "In honor of your sister?"

"Yes. It takes courage to be a warrior. Army or Marine Corps—it doesn't matter."

He nodded. "I guess we're ready."

I rode alongside Gramps. He had on his bright-red Code Talker hat with gold letters across the front—USMC.

We started out at a trot, but then we let the horses break into a smooth, loping canter. I relaxed into the motion of the horse's steady rhythm. I thought about that wild ride on Blue. How terrified I had been as we flew down the canyon, between boulders and past cotton-woods. Now those trees would be a blaze of yellow. Soon their gold would fade and the leaves would fall. One season stopped and a new one began. Like life.

Grandpa urged his horse into a gallop and pulled ahead. I leaned forward, loosened the reins, and gave a loud "*Yahoo!*" The wind dried the tears off my face and carried my words to the sky. "I miss you, Blue. Thank you for saving my life. I hope your spirit is galloping, racing wild and wonderful through those canyons with mares galore."

Our horses took off, eager to run. We were flying! Hózhǫ́ náhásdlį́į́'.

All has become beauty again.

about the navajo language

While developing the Navajo glossary for this book I have enjoyed many interesting and informative discussions, first with the late Rose A. Tahe, *Diné*, educator and reading specialist, Many Farms, Navajo Nation, Arizona; and then with Ellavina Tsosie Perkins, *Diné*, Navajo linguist, member of the Navajo Grammar Project (Navajo Language Academy); and also Mary Taylor, *Diné*, both members of the Navajo Language Renaissance Team (Rosetta Stone Endangered Languages Preservation Project).

The Navajo language has many sounds, glottal stops, and tones (high and low) that are not used in English. Thus, a simple syllable-by-syllable pronunciation guide would be inaccurate, for it could only approximate how a Navajo word or expression is pronounced. For example, the Navajo word for horse is *łį́į́*, and its correct pronunciation is nearly impossible for an English speaker. One begins to say *łį́į́* by holding the tongue near the palate and breathing out between the tongue and gums—and that's just the beginning.

The Navajo language is beautiful and unique. To learn more about the Navajo language, visit www.lapahie.com, an ongoing, evolving online dictionary. To hear spoken Navajo, listen to individual words at www.forvo.com/languages/nv. A more comprehensive online dictionary is in the works, being created by Karletta Chief, PhD, a professor at the University of Arizona and Miss Navajo Nation, 2000–2001. Rosetta Stone has a Navajo language learning text with interactive CDs.

There are many videos available online about the

Navajo language. If you search for “Navajo language” on YouTube, you’ll find videos demonstrating everything from how to say hello to the names for colors to how to start a conversation.

The Navajo language is traditionally an oral language, and although a written form was created in the 1900s, only recently have spellings, usage, and nuances of definitions been standardized, although some disagreements still continue. I have tried to use only the standardized written forms.

glossary

Bilagáana: white person

Dibé Nitsaa: Big Sheep (Hesperus Mountain, Colorado)

Diné: the people; the traditional name for Navajo

Ghąąjį’: October; time of change; the separation of summer and winter; start of the year in Navajo tradition

hastiin: term of respect for an older Navajo man; mister

hoghan: traditional home; ceremonial home; sometimes spelled hooghan

hózhǫ́: beauty around, surrounds; be in peace, in harmony; it is peaceful

hózhǫ́ náhásdlį́į́’: all has become beauty or harmony again; all is beautiful or in harmony again; it is peaceful again

kinaaldá: coming-of-age ceremony for Navajo girls

Łį́į́’ Dootł’izhii: dark horse, blue horse; depending on the light, could be gray blue

Náhookǫsjigo: toward north; toward the northern mountains

shideezhí: my younger sister

shimá sání: maternal grandmother, my mother's mother; shimá means "mother" and sání means "old"; shimá is often used alone to mean grandmother

T'áado 'áhó'ne'ída?: What is there to do?

yá'át'ééh: everyday greeting; it is good; hello!

Yé'ii: Holy Ones who return to the sacred mountains for the winter (traditionally to the San Francisco Peaks near Flagstaff, Arizona); supernatural beings

reference

Goossen, Irvy W. *Diné Bizaad: Speak, Read, Write Navajo.* Flagstaff, Arizona: Salina Bookshelf, Inc., 1995.

acknowledgments

I wish to honor Lori Piestewa, 507th Maintenance Company, US Army. Lori was born on December 14, 1979, and died on March 23, 2003, at the age of twenty-three. She was awarded the Prisoner of War Medal and the Purple Heart. Her convoy became lost and came under fire while crossing the desert in southern Iraq, just three days after the United States invaded. Lori was able to save the lives of several soldiers, including Jessica Lynch, who was captured by Iraqi soldiers and whose rescue by Navy SEALs made international news. She often described Lori as the true hero. Lori's courage and marksmanship stood out among her peers.

Lori Piestewa was a member of the Hopi tribe and was also Mexican American. She is now remembered as the first Native American woman in US history to die in combat on foreign soil while serving in the military. While her family and the citizens of Tuba City, Arizona, waited to hear news about the captive soldiers, signs were hung all around the city that said: *Put your porch light on. Show Lori the way home.* This book is dedicated to her valor, her enthusiasm for serving her country, and her dedication to family and friends.

All other characters and events in this book are fictitious, and any resemblance to real people is coincidental.

I wish to thank several Navajo elders and educators who have reviewed *Soldier Sister, Fly Home* to ensure that the Navajo culture and language are portrayed with authenticity, accuracy, sensitivity, and appropriate use. Any inaccuracies are my own. Navajo language is both precise and complex regarding names for family members. *Shimá Sání* is the official name for one's maternal grandmother. *Shimá* has become an acceptable abbreviation.

I have lived and taught on the Navajo Nation for fifteen years. It has been my privilege to share sheep camp, canyon walks, mutton stew, and lots of laughter. Thank you to the *Diné* people for your welcome.

This story was inspired by my incredible Navajo students. Sometimes they came late to class because first they needed to haul water for the sheep or give Grandma a ride to the hospital clinic, and Grandma wasn't always ready on time. Sometimes they stayed late after class because they wanted to earn a degree and feared they would never pass college algebra. And then we would talk about how weaving was mathematical, and if they talked with the instructor, maybe an extra-credit project would be an option. Perhaps something Navajo.

Thank you to those where I lived and worked for teaching me that we are alike in essential ways, and that to walk in beauty is never a race to the finish. I listened as many of my brightest students—women and men—told me they would not be in class next semester because they had decided to enlist, they knew they would be deployed, and they wanted to serve their country. I thank them for their courage.

And to my family: I would not have written my books without you. That's the truth. Thank you, Macey, for being a tough first reader; Michael and Eva, for asking for another chapter before *Soldier Sister, Fly Home*'s end; Megan and Elizabeth, for your belief that I could write this story and that it was a story worth telling; and Bill, my first editor always, even in the middle of the night, for giving me a hug and handing me a handkerchief when I'm crying. Thank you to Courageous Cookies, and especially thank you to Carolyn Lehman, Jane Resh Thomas, and Marion Dane Bauer. I especially want to acknowledge Trish Polacca for your encouragement along this journey, for reading the manuscript in between several "final" revisions, and for introducing me to the Piestewa family. And hurrah also to Trish, along with Pearl Yazzie, *Diné*, for creating a library in Tuba City that has become a community center for reading books, communication, and coming together. To Rubin Pfeffer, you believed in this story and persevered until *Soldier Sister, Fly Home* found the right home. To Yolanda Scott and Karen Boss, your insights gave both depth and polish and brought the journey to the finish line. Thank you.

The following elders and educators I especially thank for reviewing the manuscript and pointing out mistakes or misspellings of Navajo words. Any remaining errors are certainly mine. Thank you to:

Rose A. Tahe, *Diné*, educator and reading specialist, Many Farms, Navajo Nation, Arizona; Linda Ross, *Diné*, traditional healer, Chinle, Arizona; Wanda Begay, *Diné*, RN, Chinle, Arizona; Vikki Shirley, *Diné*, former first lady, Navajo Nation, regional coordinator for Arizona Reach Out and Read, Navajo Window Rock, Navajo Nation, Arizona; Ellavina Tsosie Perkins, *Diné*, Navajo linguist, member of the Navajo Grammar Project, Navajo Language Renaissance Team (Rosetta Stone Endangered Languages Preservation Project).

One more important statement of recognition and gratitude goes to the Society of Children's Book Writers and Illustrators (SCBWI). Their work to support and mentor writers is invaluable. They awarded an original version of *Soldier Sister, Fly Home* (then called *Blue*) with a Work-in-Progress Grant (multicultural) in 2012, which was a key "yes" that I needed at the time.

The Piestewa family is pleased that a percentage of the book's royalties will support the education of Lori's two children. An additional donation will be made to the American Indian College Fund (www.collegefund.org).

reader's group guide for *soldier sister, fly home*

1. Deciding on the title of a book can be difficult. When you first read the words "Soldier Sister, Fly Home" and looked at the cover, what did you expect the book to be about? What caught your attention most—a word, a phrase, or something in the image? What might you have chosen as the title? Would you have created a different cover?

2. Many of the story's themes and elements are present in the prologue, but they might not be obvious at first. After reading *Soldier Sister, Fly Home*, go back to the prologue. Can you recognize hints about the themes and elements of the book: control over one's destiny, interconnections between life and death, relationships between sisters, the importance of place and home, the internal struggle to answer "Who am I?" and "Who do I want to be?", and moral decisions about causing or preventing death? Are there other themes or elements that you see in the prologue or story?

3. In the prologue Tess says, "I swore I would never shoot a rifle again." Why does she say this? Do you think she means it? Guns, violence, and death are big worries for Tess. Later in the book Tess breaks her vow from the prologue. Why? How do you feel about her choice? Have you ever had to do something you really didn't want to do?

4. Tess feels guilty about not trying to stop the raven's death at the shooting range, and the event haunts her. Lori's death scares her. How do these feelings affect Tess's reactions when Gaby announces she is being deployed?

5. Think about some of the conversations between Tess and Gaby that show their different perspectives about being a warrior. What does it mean to each of them? To their grandfather? Why do you think the sisters feel differently about being a warrior?

6. Considering the way Tess feels about Blue, why do you think she agrees to take care of him? Why do you think Blue becomes so important to Tess?

7. What do you think is the connection between saying "yes" to taking care of Blue and "yes" to going to sheep camp? What are several possible reasons Tess agrees to both?

8. In the Navajo community the hogan is a symbol of family and home, as well as a spiritual place for ceremonies. Why is Shimá Sání's old hogan so important to her that she greets it as if welcoming an old friend?

9. In Tuba City when Tess meets her classmate Megan and Megan's cousin Rebecca, Megan asks if Tess's grandmother is a "real Indian." How does Tess answer? Later she thinks about this question and

wonders what it means to be a "real Indian." Do you think Tess's answer changes by the end of the book?

10. Shimá Sání tells Tess that "the Navajo and white are fighting inside you." What does Grandma mean when she says this to Tess? What was the purpose of the ceremony for Shimá when she returned from school as a girl, and why did the medicine man speak to her in English? Can you think of a time when you have had different parts of you fighting inside?

11. Why do you think Blue is willing to risk his own life to save Tess when the flood comes through the canyon? Do you think that moment changes Tess's view of Blue? How?

12. In the end Blue chooses to run wild rather than return to Tess. It turns out to be an important decision. Why did he do that? How have others in Tess's life also chosen a similar path? What do you think might be the outcome of those decisions?

For more questions about *Soldier Sister, Fly Home*, as well as writing prompts and other related projects, visit www.charlesbridge.com/soldiersister.